INTRODUCING ISSUES WITH OPPOSING VIEWPOINTS®

Eating Disorders

Lauri S. Friedman and Jennifer L. Skancke, *Book Editors*

GREENHAVEN PRESS
A part of Gale, Cengage Learning

GALE
CENGAGE Learning™

Detroit • New York • San Francisco • New Haven, Conn • Waterville, Maine • London

GALE
CENGAGE Learning

Christine Nasso, *Publisher*
Elizabeth Des Chenes, *Managing Editor*

For more information, contact:
Greenhaven Press
27500 Drake Rd.
Farmington Hills, MI 48331-3535
Or you can visit our Internet site at gale.cengage.com

Articles in Greenhaven Press anthologies are often edited for length to meet page requirements. In addition, original titles of these works are changed to clearly present the main thesis and to explicitly indicate the author's opinion. Every effort is made to ensure that Greenhaven Press accurately reflects the original intent of the authors. Every effort has been made to trace the owners of copyrighted material.

LIBRARY OF CONGRESS CATALOGING-IN-PUBLICATION DATA

Eating disorders / Lauri S. Friedman and Jennifer L. Skancke, book editors.
p. cm. — (Introducing issues with opposing viewpoints)
Includes bibliographical references and index.
ISBN 978-0-7377-4168-1 (hardcover)
1. Eating disorders. I. Friedman, Lauri S. II. Skancke, Jennifer.
RC552.E18E2821134 2009
616.85'26—dc22

2008026738

Printed in the United States of America
1 2 3 4 5 6 7 12 11 10 09 08

Contents

Chapter 3: How Should Web Sites That Promote Eating Disorders Be Viewed?

Foreword

Indulging in a wide spectrum of ideas, beliefs, and perspectives is a critical cornerstone of democracy. After all, it is often debates over differences of opinion, such as whether to legalize abortion, how to treat prisoners, or when to enact the death penalty, that shape our society and drive it forward. Such diversity of thought is frequently regarded as the hallmark of a healthy and civilized culture. As the Reverend Clifford Schutjer of the First Congregational Church in Mansfield, Ohio, declared in a 2001 sermon, "Surrounding oneself with only like-minded people, restricting what we listen to or read only to what we find agreeable is irresponsible. Refusing to entertain doubts once we make up our minds is a subtle but deadly form of arrogance." With this advice in mind, Introducing Issues with Opposing Viewpoints books aim to open readers' minds to the critically divergent views that comprise our world's most important debates.

Introducing Issues with Opposing Viewpoints simplifies for students the enormous and often overwhelming mass of material now available via print and electronic media. Collected in every volume is an array of opinions that captures the essence of a particular controversy or topic. Introducing Issues with Opposing Viewpoints books embody the spirit of nineteenth-century journalist Charles A. Dana's axiom: "Fight for your opinions, but do not believe that they contain the whole truth, or the only truth." Absorbing such contrasting opinions teaches students to analyze the strength of an argument and compare it to its opposition. From this process readers can inform and strengthen their own opinions, or be exposed to new information that will change their minds. Introducing Issues with Opposing Viewpoints is a mosaic of different voices. The authors are statesmen, pundits, academics, journalists, corporations, and ordinary people who have felt compelled to share their experiences and ideas in a public forum. Their words have been collected from newspapers, journals, books, speeches, interviews, and the Internet, the fastest growing body of opinionated material in the world.

Introducing Issues with Opposing Viewpoints shares many of the well-known features of its critically acclaimed parent series, Opposing Viewpoints. The articles are presented in a pro/con format, allowing readers to absorb divergent perspectives side by side. Active reading questions preface each viewpoint, requiring the student to approach the material thoughtfully and carefully. Useful charts, graphs, and cartoons supplement each article. A thorough introduction provides readers with crucial background on an issue. An annotated bibliography points the reader toward articles, books, and Web sites that contain additional information on the topic. An appendix of organizations to contact contains a wide variety of charities, nonprofit organizations, political groups, and private enterprises that each hold a position on the issue at hand. Finally, a comprehensive index allows readers to locate content quickly and efficiently.

Introducing Issues with Opposing Viewpoints is also significantly different from Opposing Viewpoints. As the series title implies, its presentation will help introduce students to the concept of opposing viewpoints and learn to use this material to aid in critical writing and debate. The series' four-color, accessible format makes the books attractive and inviting to readers of all levels. In addition, each viewpoint has been carefully edited to maximize a reader's understanding of the content. Short but thorough viewpoints capture the essence of an argument. A substantial, thought-provoking essay question placed at the end of each viewpoint asks the student to further investigate the issues raised in the viewpoint, compare and contrast two authors' arguments, or consider how one might go about forming an opinion on the topic at hand. Each viewpoint contains sidebars that include at-a-glance information and handy statistics. A Facts About section located in the back of the book further supplies students with relevant facts and figures.

Following in the tradition of the Opposing Viewpoints series, Greenhaven Press continues to provide readers with invaluable exposure to the controversial issues that shape our world. As John Stuart Mill once wrote: "The only way in which a human being can make some approach to knowing the whole of a subject is by hearing what can be said about it by persons of every variety of opinion and studying all modes in which it can be looked at by every character of mind. No wise man ever acquired his wisdom in any mode but this." It is to this principle that Introducing Issues with Opposing Viewpoints books are dedicated.

Introduction

Because eating disorders affect increasing numbers of men, women, and children each year, researchers are continually searching for clues to help them understand what causes them. They have come up with a potpourri of social, behavioral, environmental, genetic, biological, and psychological factors to explain why certain demographics of people are more likely to develop an eating disorder than others. For example, mental health experts have linked eating disorders to psychiatric conditions such as obsessive compulsive disorder (OCD), depression, and anxiety. Doctors and scientists, on the other hand, have spent years studying whether a genetic link between family members is responsible for the disordered eating habits of some sufferers. Still other researchers argue that unrealistic images of women portrayed in the media play a prominent role in dysfunctional eating behaviors.

The general consensus of those who study eating disorders is that these factors work in concert to spark the development of an eating disorder in someone. But in recent years, new research has focused on a burgeoning area of study for the development of eating disorders: whether they could possibly be brought on as a result of being sexually abused. Exploring the validity of the eating disorder–sexual abuse link may hold important clues to what causes a person to develop an eating disorder.

The loss of control one experiences when sexually abused has been suggested as the main reason why an abuse victim might develop an eating disorder later. It is thought that such people use food to assert control over their bodies in several different ways. They might subconsciously seek to become unattractive to a sexual predator by becoming too fat or too thin. Or they may be trying to punish themselves physically if they feel guilty for having "allowed" the sexual abuse to occur. Still others might be attempting to sedate themselves with food against a painful reality or to deaden terrible memories of abuse. Indeed, Diann Ackard, a Minnesota-based psychologist who works with eating disorder sufferers, has testified to the soothing power food can have for a person who has dark, painful memories of abuse. "Eating disorders can help numb intense feelings. It's like an 'anesthesia' for emotions."[1]

In addition, it is believed that victims of sexual abuse develop an eating disorder as a coping mechanism—in other words, they use an obsession with food to block out memories of past abuse. Mary Anne Cohen, director of the New York Center for Eating Disorders, says that both sexual abuse survivors and those who suffer from eating disorders share feelings of "guilt, shame, anesthesia, [and] self-punishment," and are thus all looking for "soothing, comfort, [and] protection" in food.[2] Cohen reports that 40 to 60 percent of people treated at her facility have been physically or sexually abused, convincing evidence that the link between sexual abuse and the development of an eating disorder is strong.

But not everyone is convinced that the link between sexual abuse and eating disorders is a solid one. In fact, many researchers are reluctant to say there is a direct cause-and-effect relationship between sexual abuse and eating disorders, mainly because not everyone who is sexually abused develops one. Instead, they state that the connection between the two is dependent on other present factors, such as the emotional and mental health of victims. For example, a 2005 study conducted by Anita Hund and Dorothy Espelage at the University of Illinois at Urbana-Champaign concluded that being sexually abused as a child is not enough on its own to cause a person to develop an eating disorder. The only time such abuse constitutes a significant trigger for eating disorders is when it is coupled with other psychological problems, such as depression, anxiety, or a condition called alexithymia, a disorder in which a person is unable to recognize or describe their emotions. In this case, childhood abuse victims will turn to food to express, conceal, or otherwise deal with their emotions—but the abuse alone is not enough to drive them to developing an eating disorder (as is evidenced by the fact that only some women with similar histories of sexual abuse will develop eating disorders). According to Hund, "In reality, the association between a history of childhood sexual abuse and disordered eating behaviors is very complex."[3] For these reasons, many researchers are careful to call sexual abuse a risk factor for developing eating disorders, but stop short at calling it a direct cause.

Whether there is a direct connection between sexual abuse and eating disorders may take decades to establish. But because eating disorders are a growing problem for young people in the United States, researchers are actively pursuing any and all paths that might give them clues into the causes and triggers of eating disorders. Exploring reasons why people develop eating disorders is just one of many subjects discussed in *Introducing Issues with Opposing Viewpoints: Eating Disorders.* Readers will also be introduced to articles that discuss who is at risk for eating disorders based on age, gender, and race. Experts also debate whether the media, the Internet, and peer pressure can be held accountable for the development of eating disorders. The information provided in the article pairs will help students wade through the most important issues that surround eating disorders today while pointing them in the direction of cutting-edge theories for who is at risk—and why—for developing this very serious illness.

Notes

1. Quoted in Elena Rozwadowski, "Mental Problems Often Go with Eating Disorders," *Minnesota Daily*, October 11, 2006. www.mndaily.com/articles/2006/10/11/69338.
2. Mary Anne Cohen, "Sexual Abuse and Eating Disorders," EdReferral.com, 2007. www.edreferral.com/Articles/sexualabuse&ed.htm.
3. Quoted in Craig Chamberlain, "Study Shows Complex Link Between Abuse and Eating Disorders," News Bureau, University of Illinois Urbana-Champaign, December 19, 2005. www.news.uiuc.edu/NEWS/05/1219disorders.html.

Chapter 1

Who Is at Risk for Eating Disorders?

Adolescent girls are developing eating disorders at an alarming rate, possibly to be more like their favorite celebrities.

Viewpoint 1

Adolescent Girls Are at Risk for Eating Disorders

Kristen Kemp

"Eating disorders among girls have reached all-time highs."

In the following viewpoint Kristen Kemp argues that adolescent girls are developing eating disorders at an alarming rate. She explains that during adolescence, girls feel a great deal of pressure to look a certain way, which makes them prone to developing an eating disorder. Kemp says that one reason girls have become more conscious of their weight and body size is our cultural obsession with celebrity culture. More than ever, teen girls read magazines, watch television shows, and peruse Web sites that report on what celebrities do, what they wear, and how much they weigh. Often, Kemp says, thin celebrity women are portrayed as glamorous, but in actuality they are dangerously underweight. Since teen girls look up to celebrities as people to emulate, they are increasingly turning to anorexia and bulimia in order to look like their favorite skinny celebrities.

Kemp is a writer whose work has been published in *Self, Glamour, Ladies' Home*

Kristen Kemp, "Weighing In: Girls and Weight," *Girls' Life*, vol. 12, June–July 2006, pp. 64–68.

Journal, *CosmoGIRL!*, *Marie Claire*, the *New York Daily News*, *Men's Health*, and *Girls' Life*, a magazine for girls and teens. She is also the author of twelve young adult books, fiction and nonfiction.

AS YOU READ, CONSIDER THE FOLLOWING QUESTIONS:

1. According to the author, why do many adolescent girls have poor body images?
2. What percentage of girls aged six to nineteen does the author say are overweight?
3. What does the author say is the biggest concern of teen girls during adolescence?

Everyone seems to have something to say about how girls look. Kids come up with mean names for the heavy (Miss Piggy) and the skinny (Olive Oyl). You can't even walk into a grocery store without being bombarded by tabloids that call [singer] Britney [Spears] a "post-baby porker" and [actress] Nicole Richie an "out-of-control anorexic." And then, there are the things we say to ourselves. *GL* [the magazine *Girls' Life*] surveyed hundreds of girls and found equal numbers who hate themselves for being too thin ("All my friends have something 'upstairs,' but I don't because I am so little!") and just as many who think they're too fat ("My BFF is super skinny. Next to her, I feel huge").

Is it all meaningless talk? Not exactly. The latest research on girls and weight is alarming. On one end of the scale, obesity is the No. 1 health problem for U.S. kids. On the other end, eating disorders among girls have reached all-time highs. So how did this happen?

Celebrity Worship Increases Pressure to Be Thin

The message that "thin is in" isn't a new one. But "thin" has taken on a whole new meaning: Says one *GL* reader, "My friends were in the dressing room at the mall, complaining that size 0 is too big on them. Size 0! I used to be happy being a 6, but now I feel too heavy."

To what do we owe this warped belief that humans should be in negative number sizes? "Many kids have poor body images due to the enormous pressure in celebrity culture to be super skinny," explains

Susan S. Bartell, author of *The Girls-Only Weight Loss Guide*. In the past five years, the numbers of magazines, Web sites and TV shows dedicated to celebrity worship have exploded. So girls see more images of "perfect" bodies.

[Actress] Lindsay Lohan, [singer] Hilary Duff and Nicole Richie have shed pounds—lots of them—in the past year [2006]. Their drastic weight losses haven't hurt their fan bases of mostly young girls, so these stars continue their popularity climbs. Tabloids have even reported rumors that the red string bracelet Nicole wears on her right wrist signals that she is "pro-ana," an online movement in which girls support each other's dangerous anorexic habits.

The availability of dieting tips for teens, coupled with celebrity images, causes many girls to try to obtain an unrealistic body type.

The Age of Eating Disorders

The majority of eating disorder sufferers are in their early teens and twenties, but studies have found occurrence of the disorders in children as young as six years old and in adults as old as seventy-six. Nearly two-thirds of people with eating disorders suffer from the disease for one to ten years.

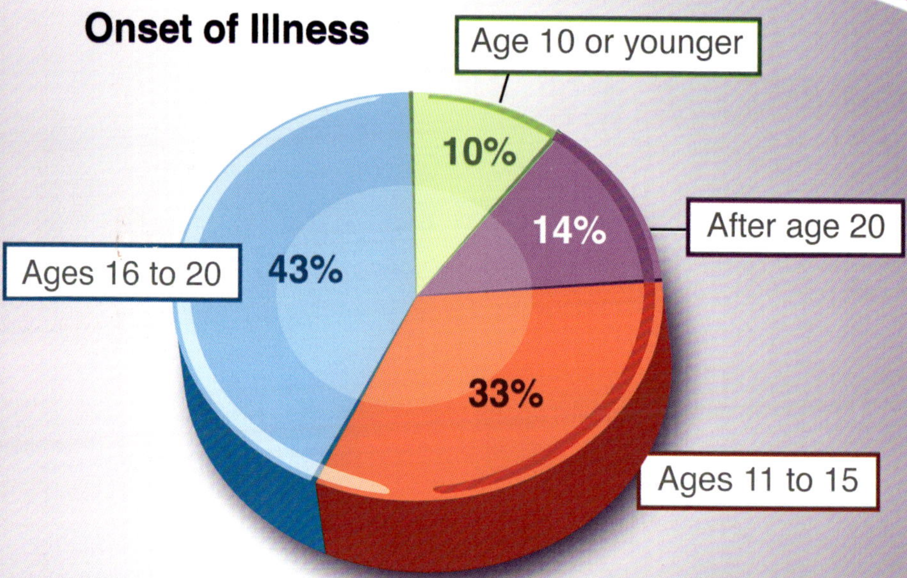

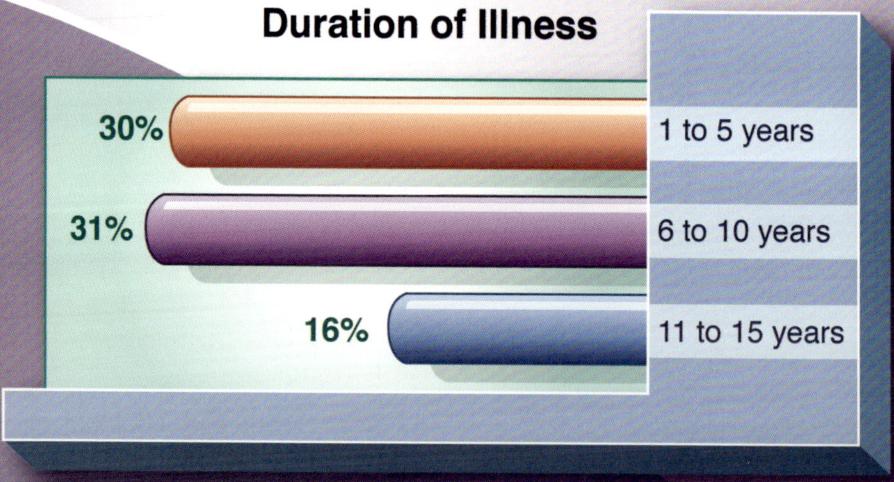

Taken from: National Association of Anorexia Nervosa and Associated Disorders.

"Many celebrities are going to even greater extremes to get noticed—personal trainers, stylists and high-priced diets are no longer enough," confesses one Hollywood-image insider, who asked us not to reveal her name because she makes her living helping teen celebs achieve an ideal she herself feels compelled to describe as "damaging."

"Stars need to set better examples, says Cheryl Dellasega, author of *Mean Girls Grown Up*. "Girls are sold on gorgeous images that aren't real and, as a result, they feel enormous pressure to look like something that's unachievable unless you have a team of professionals and digital retouching."

Fast Fact

According to the organization Anorexia Nervosa and Related Eating Disorders, Inc. (ANRED), more than 50 percent of teen girls want to lose all or some of the forty pounds gained during puberty (between eight and fourteen years old). Approximately 3 percent of these teens become anorexic or bulimic.

Adolescent Girls Are Increasingly Overweight

On the other end of the spectrum is our country's growing weight problem. Americans are literally eating themselves to death. Around the world, millions are dying because they don't have enough food. Americans are dying because we have too much. Think this only affects adults? Not so.

More U.S. teens than ever—9 million of them—are obese, according to the Centers for Disease Control. Currently, 16 percent of girls ages 6 to 19 are overweight. The American Academy of Pediatrics reports a major surge in the number of cases of Type 2 diabetes among teen girls, especially minorities. Type 2 is the kind you get when you are overweight, unlike Type 1, which happens when your body can't produce insulin. As if that weren't enough to scare you, overweight teens are now also developing diseases like hypertension, high cholesterol and weight-related asthma, conditions previously associated predominantly with adults.

Hard to believe? Not really when you consider how our lifestyles have become more butt-on-the-set (girls spend almost double the time in front of a screen from a generation ago), more inactive at school (only 28 percent of girls are required to take gym class today, down from 42 percent 15 years ago) and more dependent on processed foods (families are eating out more than ever).

Too Many Mixed Messages About Weight Contribute to Eating Disorders

Chiming in amid the worry about kids getting fat and the pressure to be thin is the "love yourself the way you are" movement. By now, everyone has seen those Dove ads (one ran during last season's Super Bowl broadcast), which encourage girls to feel good about how they look. Dove has even started The Dove Self-Esteem Fund to educate girls and women on wider definitions of beauty. Noble, sure . . . but also confusing.

Emily, 14, sums it up best: "I know it's bad to be so skinny that your bones stick out, but lots of celebrities look like that and they still get tons of attention. I know it's bad to be heavy because it's not healthy, but girls come in all shapes and sizes so I try not to judge. In school, we talk about how you should 'be happy with what you have,' but what does that mean? I felt pretty good, but I started to weigh more and my mother suddenly worried. But I wasn't eating French fries. How can I be happy when I have all this swirling around me?!?" Exactly, Emily.

The *GL* girls we surveyed tell us appearance is [their] biggest concern, even more important . . . than grades and friends. Everyone wants to be "normal," so they'll feel accepted. But how can [girls] feel normal and accepted with so many mixed messages about weight? How can [their] body's—and their self-esteem—stay strong and healthy when no one really addresses what's truly going on?

EVALUATING THE AUTHOR'S ARGUMENTS:

Kristen Kemp argues that the emphasis on celebrity in today's culture is responsible for the rise of eating disorders among adolescent girls. Clarify what she means by this, and explain what pieces of evidence she uses to support her point. Do you think she is right? Explain your answer thoroughly.

Viewpoint 2

Middle-Aged Women Are at Risk for Eating Disorders

Barbara Wingate

"One-third of inpatient [eating disorder] center admissions in 2003 were [women] over 30 years of age."

In the following viewpoint Barbara Wingate argues that middle-aged women are increasingly at risk for eating disorders. Most people associate eating disorders such as anorexia and bulimia with teenage girls and young women. However, Wingate explains that women over the age of thirty make up one-third of the population currently being treated for eating disorders. Wingate argues that middle-aged women are prone to eating disorders because they face many of the same pressures as young women to look good, and even more. A fear of aging, competition from younger women for jobs and mates, and hormonal changes all contribute to the rise of eating disorders in middle-aged women. In addition, middle-aged women experience high demands on their time from work and family, which causes them to micromanage their eating habits as a way to maintain control over their lives. The author concludes that eating disorder professionals must not

Barbara Wingate, "Mid-life Eating Eisorders and the Workplace: More and More Women Aged 30 and Older Are Presenting with Eating Disorders, and EAPs Can Play an Important Role in Minimizing the Impact on the Workplace," *The Journal of Employee Assistance,* vol. 36, January–March, 2006, pp. 9–10.

overlook middle-aged women when researching and treating eating disorders.

Wingate is medical director of Mandala Healing Center, a holistic psychiatric practice in Philadelphia. Formerly she was the medical director at the Renfrew Center, a facility devoted to the treatment of eating disorders.

AS YOU READ, CONSIDER THE FOLLOWING QUESTIONS:

1. How many women over thirty who are admitted to inpatient eating disorder centers have lifelong eating issues, according to the author?
2. What reason does Wingate give for why women over thirty with eating disorders focus on food, weight, and appearance?
3. According to the author, what characteristics are often present in the personalities of women with eating disorders?

Why is this lovely 49-year-old woman in front of me throwing up nightly?

As I listen to this well-groomed, well-spoken woman, I am trying to understand what has happened in her life that would lead her to believe and act in ways that define a clear-cut diagnosis of bulimia. Granted, all of us have complex relationships with food and eating and our body images throughout our lives. Food needs, preferences, and eating patterns start at day one; by the time we can speak, we are talking about our bodies in ways that include and exclude satisfaction with how we look and feel. Most of us do not develop eating disorders, however.

Of those who do, about 95 percent are women. Although the public associates eating disorders with teenage girls and women in their twenties, health care providers are starting to tell a different story. According to eating disorder specialist Margo Maine, Ph.D., author of *The Body Myth: The Pressure on Adult Women to Be Perfect,* one-third of inpatient center admissions in 2003 were over 30 years of age.

Increased Diagnosis of Mid-life Eating Disorders

The rise in mid-life eating disorders has significant implications for the workplace and especially for industries and professions that employ large numbers of women. But what are the underlying causes of it? Are we seeing an actual increase in mid-life eating disorders or simply an increase in diagnoses of it?

Holly Grishkat, Ph.D., who runs six inpatient groups for "over 30" women at the Renfrew Center [a facility devoted to treating eating disorders], says that about a third of them have longstanding eating issues, while slightly more had eating disorders at a younger age that went into remission but were later triggered by stress. In my own experience with this population, about half come in asking for help specifically with eating disorders and about half come in for a different reason but eventually describe symptoms severe enough to warrant an additional diagnosis.

The United States Leads the World in Eating Disorder Deaths

More deaths occur in the United States from eating disorders than in any other country in the world.

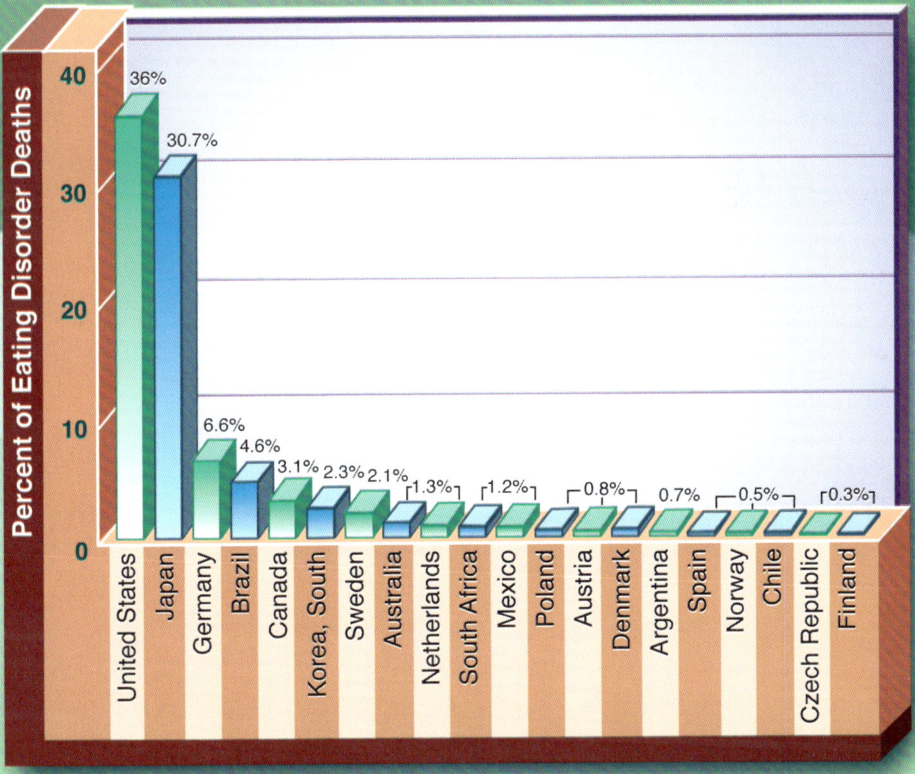

Taken from: World Health Organization and Nationmaster.com.

While younger women feel pressure to be thin and attractive, middle-aged women also often develop eating disorders to look younger and compete in the job market.

Many Reasons for Increased Mid-life Eating Disorders

Thus far, talk of eating disorders has not been backed up by research. The following information about mid-life eating disorders is largely anecdotal and attempts to explain the increased incidence we are seeing:

Fear of aging. Historically, we have not valued the older woman in American culture. Wisdom and experience do not bestow the same benefits as beauty and youth.

Competition for jobs and mates. There is evidence that jobs often go to the more attractive candidate, and attractiveness is closely related to slimness in our society. Also, because many divorces occur during mid-life years, women seeking new mates feel pressure to "spruce up" their looks by dieting.

Multiple demands and a subsequent desire for controls and rewards. The demands of work, children, spouses, personal lives, and (increasingly) aging parents can accumulate quickly and make even the most capable woman feel she is losing control. Micro-focusing on food, weight, and appearance can satisfy the need for control and can lead to food being used as an instant reward for completing tasks—with all the subsequent guilt for not maintaining control.

Hormone and metabolism changes. Women's metabolism changes during the perimenopausal years (the "bookend" to the onset of puberty), and weight gain is frequently a result. In a society that values slimness and youth, perimenopause and menopause can present a physical and psychological challenge to many women. To prevent weight gain, most women must reduce their intake of calories and exercise more frequently, including training with weights to preclude muscle loss.

Greater awareness of diet, weight, and health. Many illnesses are related to what we eat and what we weigh. As we age, we become more aware of the impact of our eating decisions. Trying to practice healthy eating habits without getting obsessed in an "eating disordered way" is important to good physical and emotional health. . . .

Symptoms of Mid-life Eating Disorders Often Hidden

The symptoms of mid-life eating disorders are likely to be hidden at work or fit within the "normal spectrum" of dieting and interest in food, weight, and appearance. In most cases, one should expect a range of experiences that are too widespread to be attributable specifically to an eating disorder. The varied diets and exercise regimens that look odd to some do not qualify as symptoms in and of themselves.

> **FAST FACT**
>
> **A 2005 study conducted by researchers at James Cook University found that disordered eating behaviors among people ages forty-five to sixty-four in Southern Australia has jumped from 11 to 28 percent since 1995.**

Some symptoms, on the other hand, resemble personality traits and behaviors that can affect relationships with co-workers. Most are not attributable to eating disorders alone but are present in a variety of problems and personalities (for instance, self-perfectionism, unrealistic expectations of others, irritability, nervousness and anxiety, lack of focus, and disorganization). The presence of an eating disorder can exacerbate any of these characteristics or behaviors.

No employee assistance professional, let alone a supervisor or manager, can simply look at someone and diagnose an eating disorder. You can estimate that someone is of excessive weight, but you cannot look at an overweight person and assume an underlying binge eating disorder. It is rare to witness dramatic symptoms such as vomiting in public bathrooms, although that is exactly how one of my patients was identified.

Even a very thin person with continued weight loss cannot be diagnosed with an eating disorder. I was involved in a case where a severely thin woman was believed by many to have an eating disorder. She claimed she could not eat without nausea, which is not an uncommon claim by anorexics; in addition, she appeared depressed. She was admitted to a psychiatric unit where I was an attending physician. After the many tests ordered by her gastroenterologist came back with normal results, a repeat set of tests revealed a pancreatic tumor. The lesson: It is important to leave diagnosing to professionals who have time, tools, and experience.

EVALUATING THE AUTHOR'S ARGUMENTS:

The author of this viewpoint, Barbara Wingate, is a former medical director at the Renfrew Center, a well-known eating disorder treatment center. Does knowing the background of the author influence your opinion of her argument? In what way?

Viewpoint 3

Adolescent Boys Are at Risk for Eating Disorders

Jenni Schaefer

"An estimated one million men in the United States suffer from an eating disorder."

In the following viewpoint Jenni Schaefer argues that teenage boys are at risk for developing an eating disorder. The author uses the story of Charles Johnson, a teenager who developed bulimia as a high school freshman, to show that eating disorders are more common in adolescent males than people think. Indeed, anorexia and bulimia are often thought of as diseases that afflict adolescent girls rather than boys, but Schaefer suggests that teenage boys face many of the same physical pressures as teenage girls. As such, the author explains they can have distorted body images, which results in the desire to lose unhealthy amounts of weight. The author concludes that these pressures can lead some boys to develop eating disorders.

Jenni Schaefer is a singer/songwriter, speaker, and author of *Life Without Ed: How One Woman Declared Independence from Her Eating Disorder and How You Can Too* (www.LifeWithoutEd.com). Appointed to the Ambassador Council of the National Eating Disorders Association, Jenni appears regularly on national radio and television to raise awareness about eating disorders and recovery.

AS YOU READ, CONSIDER THE FOLLOWING QUESTIONS:

1. According to the author, why are adolescent boys who have eating disorders ashamed to get help?
2. According to Charles Johnson, after losing his excess weight he was overcome with a fear of what?
3. After getting help for his eating disorder, Johnson realized that what characteristic or quality had contributed to the development of his bulimia?

It's no secret that girls struggle with weight issues. Models and actresses are called out in magazines for being scarily thin—and with as many as 10 million girls suffering from eating disorders in the United States, chances are you know someone with anorexia or bulimia. But what you don't hear much about is this: Guys can have eating disorders too. In fact, according to the National Eating Disorders Association, an estimated one million men in the United States suffer from an eating disorder. And since anorexia and bulimia are commonly looked at as "girl" diseases, most of those guys are too ashamed to get help, so they continue to suffer. Here is the story of one brave guy who did get help.

Pressure to Lose Weight

As a kid growing up in Media, Pennsylvania, a quaint town 20 miles from Philadelphia, I never felt like I fit in. Most people around me, including my dad, mom, and older sister, were into sports and church. Me, I was into art and music, which my dad looked down upon. I was also really shy and had trouble making friends, so after school I'd snack to pass the time until I went to bed. By fifth grade, all that snacking showed. I was chubby, and kids at school picked on me. And that just made me want to go home and eat more.

It was around then that my parents started telling me I needed to lose weight. I wanted to please them, so in sixth grade, when my dad signed

Though eating disorders are usually associated with woman and girls, at least a million American men also suffer from them.

me up to play football, I didn't resist. But it was a nightmare. I wasn't good, and the kids on the team made fun of me constantly, so about five months later I quit the team. I knew I'd disappointed my dad again.

In seventh grade, my parents separated, and as always, food helped me cope. I packed on the pounds—and the teasing got worse. One day in seventh grade, I walked into gym class and everyone started calling me fat and throwing paper at me. I ran out into the hall—and at that moment, I swore to myself that I'd lose weight.

Those with Eating Disorders Often Have a Distorted Body Image

The next day, I started jogging and cutting down on junk food. For the next year, I'd run almost every day after school. My mom, who was a jogger, encouraged me, and we'd run together sometimes.

After six months, the same kids who'd teased me started saying. "You look really good." It felt great to actually be complimented, and it motivated me to keep going. By the time I started high school in September 2002, I had lost most of my extra weight.

> **FAST FACT**
>
> **Men and boys make up approximately 5 to 15 percent of those with anorexia or bulimia, according to the National Institute of Mental Health.**

On the outside, it looked like my life was going great. The more weight I lost, the nicer kids were to me at school. I even made a few friends. But inside, I was falling apart. I was thinking about food all the time, counting the calories in everything I ate—even if it was just a cracker—and checking nutrition labels obsessively. At school, I dreaded lunch period. Afterward, I worried I'd eaten too much and couldn't wait to go home and weigh myself. My thoughts were so focused on my weight that I couldn't pay attention in class, and my grades dropped from high B's to C's. I wasn't chubby anymore, but I was so worried about being the "chubby kid" I used to be that no matter what my body looked like, I wasn't satisfied.

By junior year, I was eating almost nothing and working out every day. Then, that winter, I got a bad flu. I lost even more weight from vomiting, and it gave me the idea that I could make myself throw up. After that, bingeing and purging became a regular release for me. It wasn't just about getting food out of my body: When I purged, I felt like I was cleansing myself of anything bad that had happened that day. My mom and sister asked me a few times if I was throwing up, but I'd just lie and say no, and they'd drop it. By March 2006, my senior year, everyone around me started telling me I was too thin, but I didn't see that as a problem. Actually, it made me happy—because it meant I was still losing weight.

"My Eating Disorder Had a Lot to Do with Perfectionism"

On April 5, 2006, my 18th birthday, my mom came to me and said, "You have a problem and need help." She had set up an appointment for me at The Renfrew Center, an eating disorder clinic in Philly. I was shocked, but hearing her say it out loud made it feel real. I had a disease. I wasn't ready to get help yet, but my mom was really upset so I agreed to go. She thought I'd be more open with the doctors if I went alone, so that afternoon, I drove myself to the center. I cried the entire way; I was so afraid to face my problem. When I got there, a nurse asked me about my behaviors and attitudes toward food and my weight. Then I had my first session with my therapist, Nancy. I didn't say much—I wasn't ready to open up. But I kept seeing Nancy once a week, and after a few months, the therapy started helping. What I realized was that my eating disorder had a lot to do with perfectionism. Nothing seemed perfect in my life—like, I didn't get along with my dad and didn't have a lot of friends. I felt like if I could make my weight perfect, I'd finally do something right. Nancy helped me see how unrealistic that was. The truth is, no one can be perfect.

I continued my weekly therapy with Nancy and started college in September 2006 at the University of the Arts in Philadelphia. I felt

Males Represent a Significant Number of Patients with Eating Disorders

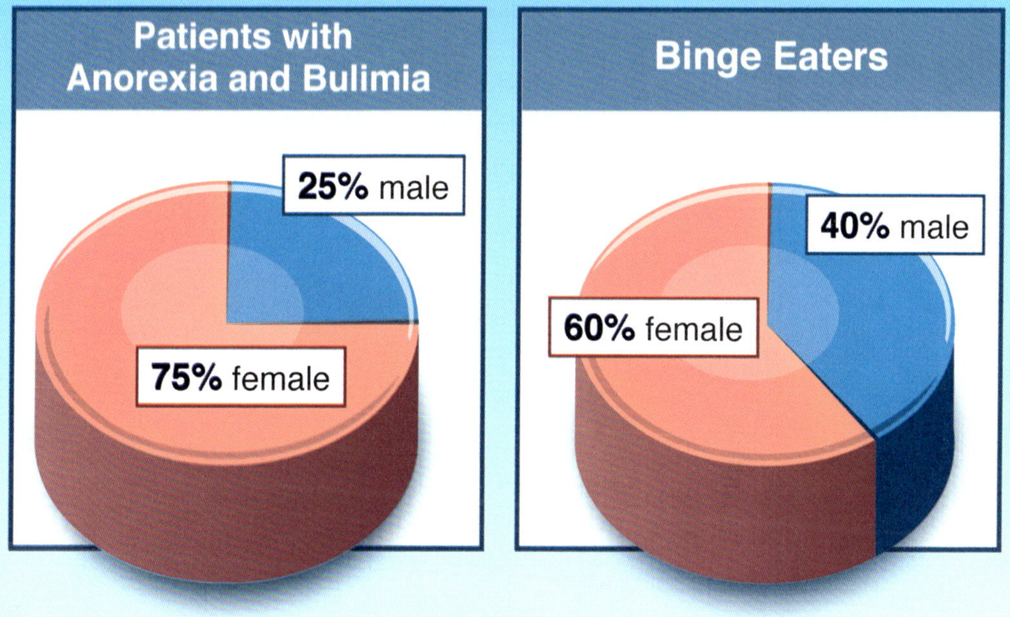

Taken from: Elizabeth Bernstein, "Men, Boys Lack Options to Treat Eating Disorders." *Wall Street Journal*, April 17, 2007.

a lot better by then—I was happier and getting healthier. But unfortunately, the stress of being in a new environment was too much for me to take, and in October I started bingeing and purging again. One night I threw up this black liquid. It freaked me out, so I went to a doctor. He said the liquid was probably excess stomach acid—and he also told me that if I lost any more weight, I could die. Those words scared me into taking my recovery—and my weekly sessions with Nancy—very seriously.

Recovering from an Eating Disorder Requires Hard Work

I'm finishing up freshman year now, and things are going great. I have friends who are really supportive, and I'm studying fashion photography, which I love. I've made a lot of progress in therapy. I know I'm not fully recovered—I still binge and purge sometimes—but I'm getting there, I don't count calories or weigh myself anymore at all. Instead of focusing on my weight, I'm focusing on my goal of becoming a professional photographer—and finally being free of my eating disorder for good.

EVALUATING THE AUTHOR'S ARGUMENTS:

Instead of relying on facts, statistics, or historical examples the way other viewpoints in this section do to make their arguments, this viewpoint focuses on the narrative story of "Charles," a teenager who has been battling an eating disorder for several years. In what ways does the narrative style differ? What advantages and disadvantage might there be in describing one person's personal story? Explain your answer thoroughly.

Viewpoint 4

White and Hispanic Women Are at Risk for Eating Disorders

"White and Hispanic girls had the highest . . . rates of EDS [Eating Disorder Symptoms]."

Katarzyna Bisaga, Agnes Whitaker, Mark Davies, Shirley Chuang, Judith Feldman, and B. Timothy Walsh

In the following viewpoint Katarzyna Bisaga, Agnes Whitaker, Mark Davies, Shirley Chuang, Judith Feldman, and B. Timothy Walsh argue that white and Hispanic women are at risk for developing eating disorders. Historically, white women have been the group most associated with eating disorders like anorexia and bulimia, the authors explain. As a group, white women show a higher incidence of eating-disordered behaviors than other ethnic groups, possibly because they are most prone to Western culture's emphasis on thinness. However, Hispanic women are increasingly assimilating, and as a result are adopting the values of white culture.

Katarzyna Bisaga, Agnes Whitaker, Mark Davies, Shirley Chuang, Judith Feldman, and B. Timothy Walsh, "Eating Disorder and Depressive Symptoms in Urban High School Girls from Different Ethnic Backgrounds," *Journal of Developmental and Behavioral Pediatrics,* vol. 26, August 2005, pp. 257–65.

This includes an increase in body dissatisfaction, which results in the development of eating disorders, according to the authors. They conclude that healthy attitudes about weight need to be promoted at a young age to help prevent eating disorders from develoing in white and Hispanic women.

Bisaga, Whitaker, Davies, Chuang, Feldman, and Walsh are medical professionals with the Child Psychiatry Division in the Department of Psychiatry at New York State Psychiatric Institute at Columbia University College of Physicians and Surgeons in New York, New York.

AS YOU READ, CONSIDER THE FOLLOWING QUESTIONS:

1. What do the authors say is one risk factor that makes white females prone to developing an eating disorder?
2. According to the authors, an association between eating disorder symptoms in Hispanic girls and what leads to problematic eating?
3. In what way do the authors say that Hispanic women's behaviors are close to those of white women's when it comes to eating disorders?

Eating disorders (ED) constitute an important source of morbidity among adolescent girls. Prevalence rates of 0.5% to 1% for anorexia nervosa and of 1% to 3% for bulimia nervosa have been reported in the United States and Europe. Moreover, the component behaviors of eating disorders (ED), such as dieting, binge eating, and self-induced vomiting are even more frequent. Eating disorder symptoms (EDS) are accompanied by depressive disorder symptoms (DDS) in both clinical and population samples.

Despite claims that in the United States, ED affect mostly non-Hispanic white females of middle class background, the balance of evidence suggests that no ethnic group is immune to eating problems, although rates vary across groups. . . . Hispanic and Native American adolescent girls and girls of East Asian descent have rates of eating problems comparable with or higher than non-Hispanic white girls. These differences in the rates of ED across minority groups in the United States raise questions regarding the specific role of ethnic background and ethnic identity as a risk and/or protective factor.

White and Hispanic Women Have Increased Rates of Eating Disorders

Attitudes toward body weight are an important aspect of a culture. For example, an endorsement of Western cultural pressures for thinness has been hypothesized as a risk factor among non-Hispanic white females. Consistent with this hypothesis, epidemiological studies have found that higher than-average body weight is associated with increased rates of dieting among non-Hispanic white adolescents and that even average weight girls diet frequently due to concerns about being overweight. Further, an association between dieting and EDS has been reported in epidemiological studies of non-Hispanic white females.

Ethnic identity has been linked to self-concept and psychological functioning of those groups whose culture is either poorly represented or discriminated against in a mainstream society. Ethnic identity has been defined as "one's sense belonging to an ethnic group and the part of one's thinking, perception, feelings, and behavior that is due to ethnic group membership." Among minority women in the United States, the endorsement of one's own ethnic background or culture of origin has a protective effect against the pressures of the dominant culture and decreases vulnerability for dieting and for ED. For example, AA [African American] adolescent girls report larger ideal body size and experience less social pressure for thinness than their non-Hispanic white counterparts, suggesting that AA cultural values offer a protective shield from pressures for thinness. Moreover, assimilation to the majority (white) culture values among AA college students was associated with more body dissatisfaction and increased rates of EDS. . . .

> **FAST FACT**
>
> Research by the U.S. Department of Health and Human Services' Office on Women's Health indicates more than 90 percent of those who suffer from eating disorders are women.

Based on the literature to date, we hypothesized that non-Hispanic white, Hispanic, and Asian girls will have higher rates of EDS, abnormal eating behaviors, and DDS [depressive disorder symptoms] than AA girls. We also hypothesized that in all ethnic except AA girls, EDS and DDS will be associated with relative body weight and abnormal eating behaviors. Finally . . . we hypothesized that a strong endorsement of ethnic identity will be associated with lower levels of EDS and DDS among all ethnic groups, whereas, conversely, a strong endorsement of the majority culture will be associated with higher levels of EDS and DDS. . . .

White and Hispanic Girls Diet at an Early Age

This study examined ethnic group status in relation to eating disorder symptoms (EDS) and depressive disorder symptoms (DDS) in urban adolescent girls. The associations of ethnic identity, relative body weight, and abnormal eating behaviors with EDS and DDS across ethnic groups were also assessed.

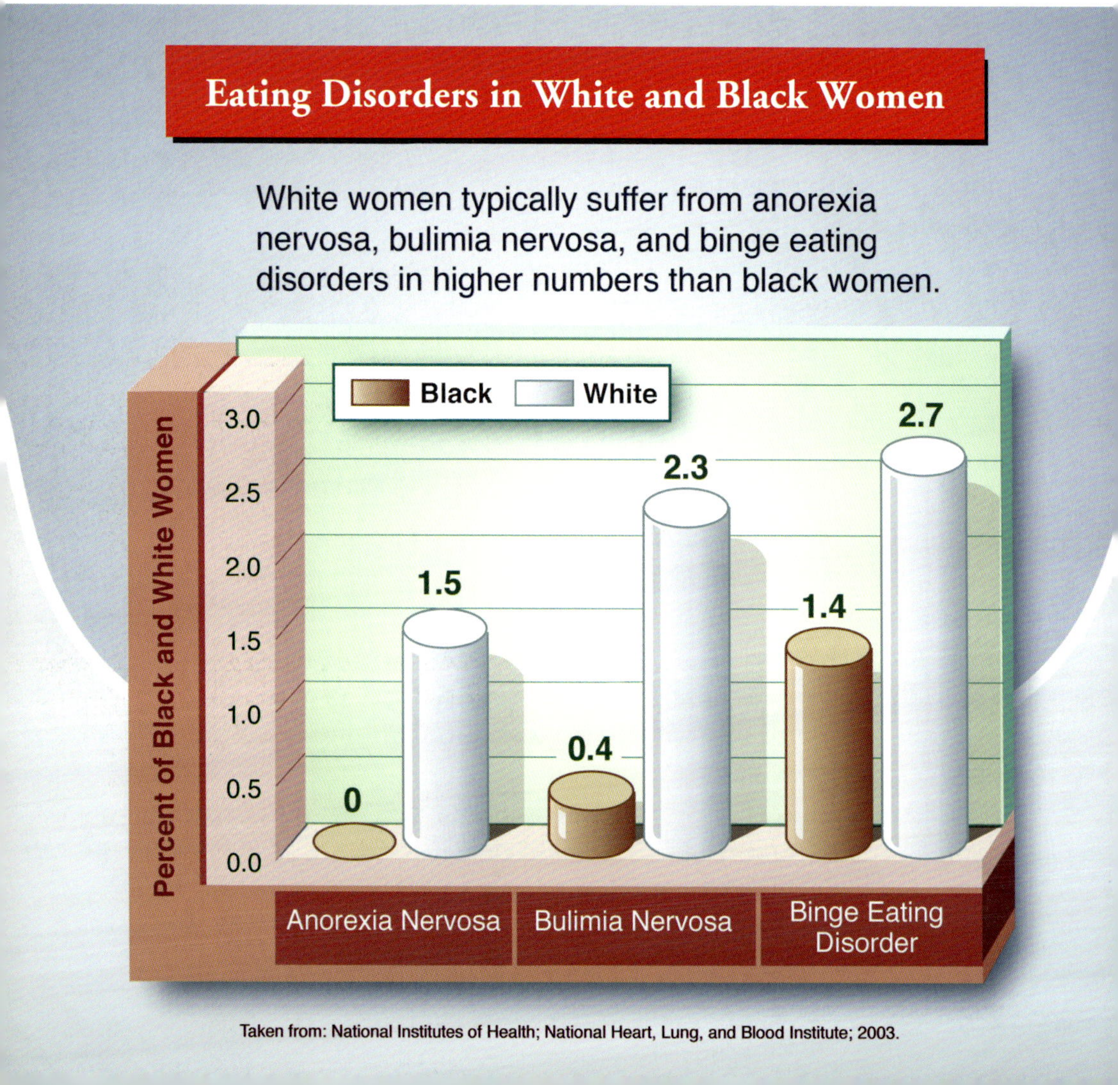

Our results confirm that no ethnic group is immune to EDS and DDS and that there are important ethnic group differences in the rates of these two types of symptoms. As hypothesized non-Hispanic white and Hispanic girls had the highest and African-American (AA) and Caribbean girls the lowest rates of EDS. Our findings, both with respect to EDS and abnormal eating behaviors are similar to those of previous epidemiological studies in which AA and Caribbean girls reported low rates of EDS and started dieting later.

Non-Hispanic white girls reported high rates of EDS similar to other epidemiological studies. Hispanic girls also reported high rates of EDS, similar to the findings of [researchers D. A.] Pastore et al in metropolitan Hispanic youths. They started dieting, engaged in self-induced vomiting, and used diet pills at an earlier age than Caribbean and AA girls. These findings add to the accumulating evidence that Hispanic girls are at high risk of eating disorders (ED). Hispanic girls reported rates of DDS similar to non-Hispanic white girls. [Researchers] [J.M.] Twenge and [S.] Nolen-Hoeksema described rates of depression among Hispanic adolescents to be higher than among non-Hispanic white or AA youths, but others found no differences. This might be due to sampling methods because both our sample and that of [researchers G. J.] Emslie et al were derived from high school youths, whereas others studied middle school youths.

Abnormal Eating Is Disproportional to Body Weight

The girls with mixed ethnic background had rates of dieting, fasting, and diet pill and laxative use comparable with those of other groups with the exception of self-induced vomiting, for which the rate was surprisingly high. Interpreting results for the mixed background group poses a dilemma given that it was composed of girls who self-identified as members of at least two groups. As mentioned earlier, the majority in this group had one non-Hispanic white parent, which may affect an increased vulnerability to the pressures of majority culture. . . .

With respect to the relation of relative body weight to EDS and DDS, we found, contrary to our expectation, important ethnic differences. In our study, Hispanic and Asian girls showed significantly stronger correlation between body mass index (BMI) and EDS than non-Hispanic whites. Others also found that among non-Hispanic white girls, abnormal eating is often disproportional to body weight. An association between BMI and EDS in Hispanic girls suggests that higher BMI contributes to problematic eating. Indeed, Hispanic adolescent girls report high body dissatisfaction, and Hispanic adult women report high discrepancy between the actual and desired weight.

Among non-Hispanic whites and mixed background girls there was a weak positive correlation between BMI and DDS, suggesting a possible role of body weight in generating DDS.

Western Culture Emphasizes Thinness

In our school-based sample, early dieting was the only abnormal eating behavior associated with current EDS and DDS. A recent epidemiological prospective study found that medically unsupervised dieting among adolescents was associated with weight gain. Dieting as a risk factor for EDS has been previously described in population studies of non-Hispanic white girls. . . . Our finding of an association between early dieting and DDS among non-Hispanic white and mixed background girls, independent of weight, indicates that early unsupervised dieting might contribute to the development of depressive symptoms among adolescent girls. This finding suggests that Western cultural pressures for thinness may play a role not only in the development of EDS but also in the development of DDS in adolescence. . . .

Our expectation that high endorsement of the majority culture will be associated with increased level of symptoms was supported because high other group orientation scores were associated with EDS in Hispanic and mixed background girls and with DDS in the total sample. The former finding is consistent with suggestions that Hispanic girls may be more vulnerable to the pressures of the majority culture than AA girls. For example, Hispanic girls identify with the majority culture media images, which are not viewed as role models by AA girls. As mentioned earlier, the mixed background group was ethnically heterogeneous and possibly susceptible to the influence of other groups and the majority culture. This observation could also explain an association of high other group orientation with DDS in our sample. Alternatively, strong interest in other ethnic groups might signify the adolescent identity confusion associated with distress and depressed mood.

Developing Preventive Programs Is Necessary

In summary, our findings underscore the importance of ethnic group status with regards to BMI, EDS, and DDS. We found the highest rates of EDS in non-Hispanic white and Hispanic girls and the lowest rates in AA and Caribbean girls. Asian girls had the highest rates of DDS, whereas AA girls had the lowest rates. Ethnic identity achievement was not associated with psychological outcomes; however, high other group orientation was related to both EDS and

By promoting a positive body image and instilling healthy eating habits in their children, parents can prevent the development of eating disorders.

DDS. Significant ethnic group differences in the rates of EDS and DDS might be related to ethnic group differences in BMI and in attitudes toward weight. Early unsupervised dieting was associated with increased rates of EDS and DDS among non-Hispanic white, Caribbean, and mixed background girls.

Parents and educators may play an important role in promoting healthy attitudes toward body weight. Preventive strategies should focus on healthy eating habits and emphasize that unsupervised dieting may pose a risk for EDS and DDS among both average and higher-than-average weight adolescent girls. Primary care clinicians working with ethnically diverse youths should inquire about EDS and DDS. Our findings also point to the need for the development of ethnically sensitive assessment and treatment methods for EDS and DDS.

EVALUATING THE AUTHORS' ARGUMENTS:

In the viewpoint you just read, the authors use research and statistics to make their argument that white and Hispanic women are at risk for developing eating disorders. They do not, however, use any quotes to support their point. If you were to rewrite this article and insert quotations, what authorities might you quote from? Where would you place these quotes to bolster the authors' points?

Chapter 2

What Contributes to the Development of Eating Disorders?

The media often portrays underweight celebrities as the "norm," which leads many girls and women to turn to eating disorders to become thin.

Viewpoint 1

The Media Causes Eating Disorders

Janine K. van Nostrand

"Images of excessively thin models in magazines and television led to an increase in eating disorders."

In the following viewpoint Janine K. van Nostrand argues that media images and advertising cause eating disorders. Magazines, television, and movies bombard Americans with pictures of incredibly thin models and celebrities, she argues. The media commonly show underweight women as being the "norm" for body size, which affects women's and girls' body images. They internalize these images and begin to think that they too must look like thin celebrities in order to be considered beautiful. To reach this unobtainable body size, they turn to anorexia or bulimia. The author concludes by saying that the media needs to be held accountable for its role in encouraging society's unhealthy obsession with thinness and do its part to reduce the occurrence of eating disorders.

Van Nostrand graduated from Lehigh University with a BA in journalism. She currently resides in Long Island, New York, where she works as a paralegal.

Janine K. van Nostrand, "The Media Contributes to Eating Disorders." The original article appeared online as a George Washington University Conference Paper, February 2008. This updated version of the original article has been reproduced by permission of the author.

AS YOU READ, CONSIDER THE FOLLOWING QUESTIONS:

1. What does the author say is the number one wish of girls ages eleven to seventeen?
2. According to Van Nostrand, what message do magazines send to readers when they only portray "picture-perfect bodies?"
3. How do the number of weight-loss advertisements in women's magazines compare to those found in men's magazines, according to the author?

"It was kind of boring for me to have to eat. I would know that I had to, and I would." —Kate Moss

The words "eat" and "boring" are usually never found in the same sentence, but leave it to a supermodel to accomplish this task. Bodies reminiscent of the Holocaust, clad only in a bathing suit, underwear, or a skimpy tank top, flood popular fashion magazines today. How many times have you flipped through the pages of your favorite magazine and spotted an article about how women should have a good perception of themselves, how they should "celebrate those curves," and then turned the page to find a centerfold makeover section complete with before and after pictures?

As a girl enters puberty, the changes in her physical appearance can result in feelings of confusion and angst. She becomes highly susceptible to social influences, fearful of not fitting in with her peers. During this time, it is much more difficult for her to realize that making her own body look like those of the girls she sees in commercials and magazine ads is impossible unless she develops severely disordered eating habits. Here are some statistics found on the Eating Disorders Coalition Web site: 51% of 9- [and] 10-year-old girls feel better when they're dieting; 81% of 10-year-old girls are afraid of being fat; 53% of 13-year-old girls are unhappy with their bodies; and 78% of 18-year-old girls are unhappy with their bodies. The most striking reality: the number one wish of girls ages 11–17 is to lose weight.

Images in Magazines Affect Girls' Body Images

Sufferers of eating disorders have admitted that images of skinny models enflamed their condition. The fashion industry does not present a

Unrealistic Body Images

The table below compares the dimensions of the average American woman with the dimensions of Barbie dolls and department store mannequins. Barbie's dimensions are so unrealistic, if she were a real woman, her neck would be too long and thin to support her head, and her upper body proportions would make it difficult for her to walk upright. Both Barbie and store mannequins do not reflect the dimensions of average women.

	Average Woman	Barbie	Store Mannequin
Height	5'4"	7'2"	6'0"
Weight	145 lbs.	101 lbs.	Not available
Dress Size	11–14	4	6
Bust	36–37"	39"	34"
Waist	29–31"	18"	23"
Hips	40–42"	33"	34"

Taken from: *Health*, September 1997; National Eating Disorder Information Centre; K.D. Brownell and M.A. Napolitano, "Distorting Reality for Children: Body Size Proportions of Barbie and Ken Dolls," *International Journal of Eating Disorders*, vol. 18, no. 3, 1995, pp. 295–98.

realistic view of women to the public. People come in all shapes and sizes. How many times have you heard that statement? It seems obvious, no? Then why is it that all the models strutting down the runways at Fashion Week, or modeling the top designers' collections in magazine ads are all so thin that you can see their bones jutting out of their skin? The average American woman is 5'4" and weighs 140 pounds. The average American model is 5'11" and weighs 117 pounds. That means models are thinner than 98% of all American women.

In Sharlene Hesse-Biber's book, *Am I Thin Enough Yet?*, college girls explain how the influence of the magazines they read affects their body image. One college senior, Delia, explains, "I am so affected by *Glamour* magazine and *Vogue*. . . . I'm looking at these beautiful women. They're thin. I want to be. . . ." Another college student expresses the same feeling: "I would see these thin girls in the magazines and say I want to be like that. I would look at myself in the mirror and didn't like what I saw." With the increasing bombardment of these advertisements, it is no surprise that girls have resorted to eating disorders to conform to the hidden message sent by the fashion industry: thin is in.

Fashion editors should realize that by presenting picture perfect bodies throughout their magazines, they are sending a certain message to their readers, especially when their target audience is vulnerable teenage girls. If teens are surrounded solely by these images in their everyday lives, they will begin to believe that they must look the same way. Editors maintain, however, that the idea of their advertisements provoking disordered eating habits amongst their readers is ridiculous. They feel that they are simply responding to a "supply and demand" phenomenon, and what is in demand at photo shoots and fashion shows is one of those 5'11", 117-pound "average" American models.

Magazines Have the Power to Influence Women

As the fashion industry rapidly underwent several changes throughout the twentieth century, fashion magazines and advertisers had a field day with the new material to bring to the public's eye. Fashion trends throughout history have been one of the primary focuses of content for the media. We forget that the period of time between the 1940s and 1960s did not involve personal computers, the Internet, cable television or DVD players. Magazines had a much greater role during this era. They shaped and reflected the values, habits and aspirations of American women with incredible circulation. *Harper's Bazaar* and *Vogue* have been influencing American women since they were established in the

Fast Fact

According to the National Institute on Media and the Family, 37 percent of the articles featured in popular teen girl magazines include some focus on appearance, and 50 percent of ads use beauty to sell their products.

late 1800s. Women did not only read the pages of these magazines, but scrutinized them. Fashion magazines were studied intensively and influenced the clothes, the activities and the thoughts of women.

Diet and Beauty Advertisements Are Misleading

Today [2008] we face such incredible advances in digital technology and their effects on magazine ads. We don't know what is real anymore in the ads that we see. Images are airbrushed, wrinkles are erased and blemishes disappear with the touch of a button. Our perception of reality is shaped by how computer graphics specialists interpret and portray their own ideas of reality onto us. Think of all the manipulation that goes into one of the many advertisements found in a fashion magazine. Then think of how many pages of that same fashion magazine are actually advertisements. Women's magazines contain 10.5 times more articles and ads related to dieting and weight loss than men's magazines, and for every one advertisement related to dieting seen in an issue of a men's magazine, there are sixty-three in magazines read by women.

The editors and computer graphics artists who feel you cannot catch an eating disorder from the pages of a magazine ignore the fact that adolescence is one of the most vulnerable stages in your life; the sudden physical and hormonal changes one's body undergoes leave a teenager confused and often diminish their body image. Adolescents strive to fit in with their peers at large and become more susceptible to ad persuasion. With an estimated 60% of girls reading at least one fashion magazine regularly, persuasion can become overpowering. Results of a 1990 study showed that all subjects involved experienced the greatest pressure to be thin from the media. Exposure to the thin ideal portrayed can cause depression, shame, guilt, body dissatisfaction and stress. Digital technology has only added to the controversy. It becomes impossible to distinguish from what is real and what has been digitally altered in magazines, and teenagers feel pressure to transform their bodies to match those of 5'10", 97-pound model Kate Moss.

The Media Should Promote Honest Images of Beauty

In a society where everyone is surrounded by advertising from childhood and where it is a part of everyday life, it would be unrealistic to tell someone to stop reading magazines or watching television. That is not the solution to this ongoing problem. The media needs to focus on an honest and real concept of beauty that is based on diversity of shape. Cover stories of fashion and entertainment magazines don't always have to be about the latest celebrity who dropped all her baby

Many people feel that the media should be more responsible in marketing celebrities and unrealistic body images.

weight in record time, or ridiculing the celebrity who has put on a few pounds.

In June 2000, the British Government held a Body Image Summit to address concerns that images of excessively thin models in magazines and television led to an increase in eating disorders. The seminar was led by British politician Tessa Jowell. At the summit, Jowell urged fashion editors to stop using "very thin girls with protruding bones" in their ads and articles. Susie Orbach, the therapist who treated the late Princess Diana for her bulimia, suggested that modeling agencies and fashion designers could set aside profits for fashion students who promote gorgeous clothes in all sizes. Such seminars and open discussions need to be brought into the United States. Fashion designers, advertisers and editors should assume more responsibility for the role they play in influencing vulnerable teenage girls' perception of what society deems acceptable. There should be more realistic models to boost readers' confidence rather than crush it. Media has become a very powerful and manipulative tool in today's world. It should be their responsibility to stop feeding their readers unrealistic views of acceptable body image and start acknowledging the startling facts and statistics about eating disorders.

EVALUATING THE AUTHOR'S ARGUMENTS:

In the viewpoint you just read, the author suggests the media should take responsibility for the unrealistic images it presents to women and girls. What do you think? Should the media choose more realistically sized models, or should viewers take responsibility for what they read and watch? Explain your position.

Viewpoint 2

The Media Does Not Cause Eating Disorders

SomethingFishy.org

"The media most certainly contributes to dieting and size discrimination, but eating disorders are not diets!"

In the following viewpoint SomethingFishy.org argues that the media is not responsible for causing eating disorders. The author admits that the media places a strong emphasis on beauty and dieting in America by favoring images of models and actresses. However, the media alone does not drive someone to become anorexic or bulimic. Magazines, television, newspapers, and movies are reviewed by millions of Americans, yet just a small percentage of them will develop an eating disorder. If an individual is susceptible to an eating disorder, the author claims, he or she will suffer from it regardless of the media's messages about weight and body image. More important causes of eating disorders include genetics, stress, environment, alcoholism, drug abuse, and depression. The author concludes that these reasons are more to blame for eating disorders than media images.

SomethingFishy.org, "The Media: Exploring the Role Society and the Media Play in the Development of an Eating Disorder and the Media Influence on Eating Disorders," 2007. http://somethingfishy.org. Used by permission of CRC Health.

SomethingFishy.org is a comprehensive Web site that provides information and support for sufferers, friends, and families of sufferers of anorexia, bulimia, compulsive overeating, and binge-eating disorders.

AS YOU READ, CONSIDER THE FOLLOWING QUESTIONS:

1. What percentage of the world's population has an eating disorder, according to the author?
2. According to the author, how does the diet industry contribute to society's beliefs about body image?
3. To what extent does the author believe a preoccupation with weight and food results in the development of an eating disorder?

Okay, so we all want to hear how Calvin Klein is the culprit and that the emaciated waif look has caused women to tailspin into the world of eating disorders. While the images of child-like women has obviously contributed to an increased obsession to be thin, and we can't deny the media influence on eating disorders, there's a lot more to it than that. With approximately six billion people in the world, and a mere ten million of them suffering with some type of disordered eating (.18% of the overall population—less than a 1/4 of 1%), the media obviously doesn't cause *everyone* to develop anorexia, bulimia or compulsive overeating. (Current statistics indicated that approximately one in every one hundred teenage girls may develop an Eating Disorder.)

It is a lot more complex than blaming the media. The media most certainly contributes to dieting and size discrimination but eating disorders are not diets!

The Media Contributes to Dieting, Not Eating Disorders

From early-on children are taught by society that their looks matter. Think of the three and four year old who is continuously praised for being "oh so cute." With an increased population of children who spend a lot of time in front of television, there are more of them coming up with a superficial sense of who they are. Images on T.V. spend countless hours telling us to lose weight, be thin and beautiful, buy more stuff because people will like us and we'll be better people for it. Programming on the tube rarely depicts men and women with "average" body-types or crappy clothes, ingraining in the back of all our minds that this is the type of life we want. Overweight characters are typically portrayed as lazy, the one with no friends, or "the bad guy," while thin women and pumped-up men are the successful, popular, sexy and powerful ones. How can we tell our children that it's what's inside that counts, when the media continuously contradicts this message?

Despite constant publicity of "anorexic looking" models and celebrities, the media is not the only factor in the development of eating disorders. Stress, mental illness, and genetics can also play a role.

Images in Magazines Are Fake

Super models in all the popular magazines have continued to get thinner and thinner. Modeling agencies have been reported to actively pursue anorexic models. The average woman model weighs up to 25% less than the typical woman and maintains a weight at about 15 to 20 percent below what is considered healthy for her age and height. Some models go through plastic surgery, some are "taped-up" to mold their bodies into more photogenic representations of themselves, and photos are airbrushed before going to print. By far, these body types and images are not the norm and unobtainable to the average individual, and far and wide, the constant force of these images on society makes us believe they should be. We need to

Causes of Eating Disorders

A 2006 poll by the National Eating Disorders Association (NEDA) of American college students found the following were most commonly given as causes of eating disorders:

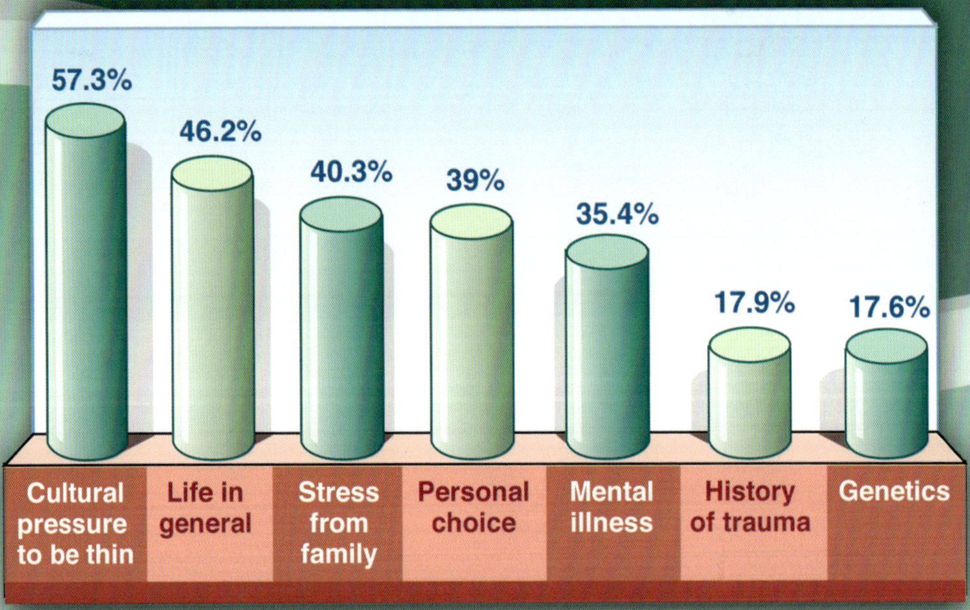

*Answers do not total 100% because respondents gave more than one answer.

Taken from: National Eating Disorders Association, September 26, 2006.

remind ourselves and each other constantly (especially children) that these images are *fake.*

Advertisements Make False Claims About Beauty

Diet advertisements are another problem. On television, in magazines and newspapers, we are continually exposed to the notion that losing weight will make us happier and it will be through "*This* diet plan." Time and time again it has been proven that, for the long-term, regimented diet plans *do not* work, yet our society continues to buy into the idea that they do. Pop-culture's imposed definition of "the ideal body" combined with the diet industry's drive to make more money, creates a never-ending cycle of ad upon ad that try to convince us ". . . If you lose weight, your life will be good." The flip side is that as long as we continue to buy into their false claims by purchasing these (often dangerous) products, the more the diet industry will keep pushing their slogans at us.

FAST FACT

According to the Mayo Clinic, anorexia and other eating disorders existed centuries ago—long before modern media—which suggests "sociocultural values" are not solely to blame.

From the About-Face organization: "400–600 advertisements bombard us everyday in magazines, on billboards, on tv, and in newspapers. One in eleven has a direct message about beauty, not even counting the indirect messages."

The Media Does Not Cause Eating Disorders

While all of these images, advertisements, and messages may be counterproductive to a good self-image, and society's overall acceptance of each person's different size and shape, they are *not* the reason so many men and women develop an eating disorder. These images may not help, and for those already open to the possibility of negative coping mechanisms and/or mental illness, the media may play a small contributing role—but ultimately, if a young man or woman's life situation, environment, and/or genetics leave them open to an eating disorder (or alcoholism, drug abuse, depression, OCD, etc.), they will still end up in the same place *regardless of television or magazines.* Ultimately it's important to know that anorexia, bulimia and compulsive overeating are *not* about weight and food. Rather they are complex disorders where each sufferer is plagued with low self-esteem, an inability to cope with their own emotions and stress, and many underlying issues that have led them to their disordered eating.

EVALUATING THE AUTHORS' ARGUMENTS:

In this viewpoint the author argues that magazines, television, and the Internet do not directly cause eating disorders. The author of the previous viewpoint, Janine K. van Nostrand, says that these media outlets play a direct role in eating disorders by promoting and encouraging a false ideal of thinness. With which author's perspective do you agree? Why?

Viewpoint 3

Biological and Psychological Factors Cause Eating Disorders

"Scientists and doctors think of eating disorders as medical illnesses with certain biological causes."

National Institute of Mental Health

In the following viewpoint the National Institute of Mental Health argues that biological and psychological factors contribute to the development of eating disorders. The root cause of eating disorders lies in the human brain, the authors claim. For unknown reasons, the brains of individuals with eating disorders develop abnormal thinking and processing patterns, which often manifest as severe disturbances in eating behavior. Some of these behaviors include excessive overeating, extreme portion control, self-induced vomiting, and a distorted body image. The authors explain that these eating behaviors usually coexist in conjunction with other mental disorders like depression, substance abuse, and anxiety disorders. The National Institute of Mental Health concludes that eating disorders are caused by complex biological and

National Institute of Mental Health (NIMH), "Eating Disorders," 2007.

psychological factors and more research is needed to better understand the relationship.

The National Institute of Mental Health is the largest scientific organization in the world dedicated to understanding, treating, and preventing mental disorders, including eating disorders.

AS YOU READ, CONSIDER THE FOLLOWING QUESTIONS:

1. According to the authors, eating disorders often coexist with what other psychiatric disorders?
2. What is neuroimaging, as described by the authors?
3. Anorexics are how many more times likely to die than non-anorexics, according to the National Institute of Mental Health?

An eating disorder is marked by extremes. It is present when a person experiences severe disturbances in eating behavior, such as extreme reduction of food intake or extreme overeating, or feelings of extreme distress or concern about body weight or shape.

A person with an eating disorder may have started out just eating smaller or larger amounts of food than usual, but at some point, the urge to eat less or more spirals out of control. Eating disorders are very complex, and despite scientific research to understand them, the biological, behavioral and social underpinnings of these illnesses remain elusive.

Eating Disorders Are Medical Illnesses

The two main types of eating disorders are anorexia nervosa and bulimia nervosa. A third category is "eating disorders not otherwise specified (EDNOS)," which includes several variations of eating disorders. Most of these disorders are similar to anorexia or bulimia but with slightly different characteristics. Binge-eating disorder, which has received increasing research and media attention in recent years, is one type of EDNOS.

Eating disorders frequently appear during adolescence or young adulthood, but some reports indicate that they can develop during childhood or later in adulthood. Women and girls are much more likely than males to develop an eating disorder. Men and boys account for an estimated 5 to 15 percent of patients with anorexia or bulimia and an estimated 35 percent of those with binge-eating disorder.

Eating disorders are real, treatable medical illnesses with complex underlying psychological and biological causes. They frequently co-exist with other psychiatric disorders such as depression, substance abuse, or anxiety disorders. People with eating disorders also can suffer from numerous other physical health complications, such as heart conditions or kidney failure, which can lead to death. . . .

Anorexics Are Obsessed with Weight Control

Anorexia nervosa is characterized by emaciation, a relentless pursuit of thinness and unwillingness to maintain a normal or healthy weight, a distortion of body image and intense fear of gaining weight, a lack of menstruation among girls and women, and extremely disturbed eating behavior. Some people with anorexia lose weight by dieting and exercising excessively; others lose weight by self-induced vomiting, or misusing laxatives, diuretics or enemas.

> **FAST FACT**
>
> **According to the University of Maryland Medical Center, obsessive compulsive disorder is present in up to two-thirds of those who suffer from anorexia.**

Many people with anorexia see themselves as overweight, even when they are starved or are clearly malnourished. Eating, food and weight control become obsessions. A person with anorexia typically weighs herself or himself repeatedly, portions food carefully, and eats only very small quantities of only certain foods.

Some who have anorexia recover with treatment after only one episode. Others get well but have relapses. Still others have a more chronic form of anorexia, in which their health deteriorates over many years as they battle the illness.

According to some studies, people with anorexia are up to ten times more likely to die as a result of their illness compared to those without the disorder. The most common complications that lead to death are cardiac arrest, and electrolyte and fluid imbalances. Suicide also can result.

American Attitudes About Eating Disorders

National surveys reveal that Americans think eating disorders are serious diseases, but less than half are familiar with specific disorders and their health effects.

Do you think eating disorders are serious illnesses?

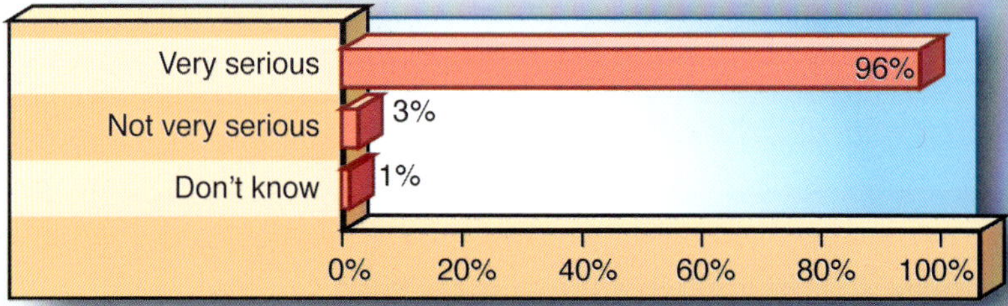

Please check which of the following eating disorders, if any, you are familiar with:

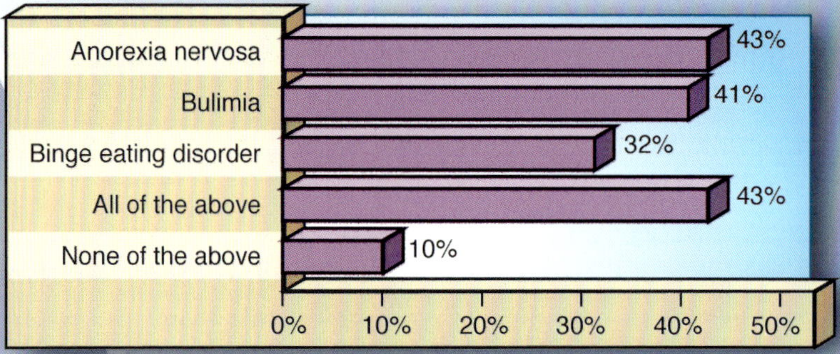

Which of the following health complications do you believe could be the result of an eating disorder?

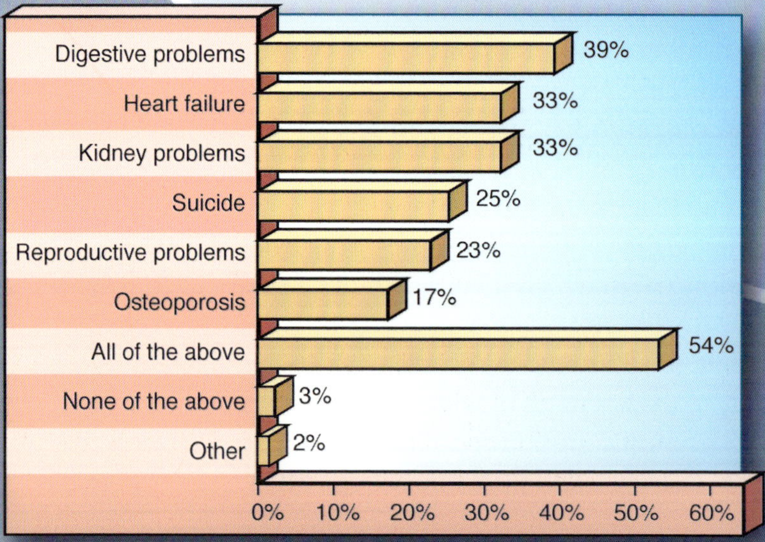

Taken from: National Eating Disorders Association (NEDA) and GMI, Inc., 2005.

Many people with anorexia also have coexisting psychiatric and physical illnesses, including depression, anxiety, obsessive behavior, substance abuse, cardiovascular and neurological complications, and impaired physical development. . . .

Bulimia Sparks Feelings of Disgust and Shame

Bulimia nervosa is characterized by recurrent and frequent episodes of eating unusually large amounts of food (e.g., binge-eating), and feeling a lack of control over the eating. This binge-eating is followed by a type of behavior that compensates for the binge, such as purging (e.g., vomiting, excessive use of laxatives or diuretics), fasting and/or excessive exercise.

Unlike anorexia, people with bulimia can fall within the normal range for their age and weight. But like people with anorexia, they often fear gaining weight, want desperately to lose weight, and are intensely unhappy with their body size and shape. Usually, bulimic behavior is done secretly, because it is often accompanied by feelings of disgust or shame. The binging and purging cycle usually repeats several times a week.

Similar to anorexia, people with bulimia often have coexisting psychological illnesses, such as depression, anxiety and/or substance abuse problems. Many physical conditions result from the purging aspect of the illness, including electrolyte imbalances, gastrointestinal problems, and oral and tooth-related problems. . . .

Binge-Eaters Feel a Loss of Control

Binge-eating disorder is characterized by recurrent binge-eating episodes during which a person feels a loss of control over his or her eating. Unlike bulimia, binge-eating episodes are not followed by purging, excessive exercise or fasting. As a result, people with binge-eating disorder often are overweight or obese. They also experience guilt, shame and/or distress about the binge-eating, which can lead to more binge-eating.

Obese people with binge-eating disorder often have coexisting psychological illnesses including anxiety, depression, and personality disorders. In addition, links between obesity and cardiovascular disease and hypertension are well documented. . . .

Boys with Eating Disorders Exhibit Emotional and Behavioral Symptoms

Although eating disorders primarily affect women and girls, boys and men are also vulnerable. One in four preadolescent cases of anorexia occurs in boys, and binge-eating disorder affects females and males about equally.

Like females who have eating disorders, males with the illness have a warped sense of body image and often have muscle dysmorphia, a type of disorder that is characterized by an extreme concern with becoming more muscular. Some boys with the disorder want to lose weight, while others want to gain weight or "bulk up." Boys who think they are too small are at a greater risk for using steroids or other dangerous drugs to increase muscle mass.

Boys with eating disorders exhibit the same types of emotional, physical and behavioral signs and symptoms as girls, but for a variety of reasons, boys are less likely to be diagnosed with what is often considered a stereotypically "female" disorder.

Individuals with Eating Disorders Have Abnormal Brain Activity

Researchers are unsure of the underlying causes and nature of eating disorders. Unlike a neurological disorder, which generally can be pinpointed to a specific lesion on the brain, an eating disorder likely involves abnormal activity distributed across brain systems. With increased recognition that mental disorders are brain disorders, more researchers are using tools from both modern neuroscience and modern psychology to better understand eating disorders.

One approach involves the study of the human genes. With the publication of the human genome sequence in 2003, mental health researchers are studying the various combinations of genes to determine if any DNA variations are associated with the risk of developing a mental disorder. Neuroimaging, such as the use of magnetic resonance imaging (MRI), may also lead to a better understanding of eating disorders.

Neuroimaging already is used to identify abnormal brain activity in patients with schizophrenia, obsessive-compulsive disorder and depression. It may also help researchers better understand how people with eating disorders process information, regardless of whether they have recovered or are still in the throes of their illness.

Conducting behavioral or psychological research on eating disorders is even more complex and challenging. As a result, few studies of treatments for eating disorders have been conducted in the past. New studies currently underway, however, are aiming to remedy the lack of information available about treatment.

Eating Disorders Have Biological and Psychological Causes

Researchers also are working to define the basic processes of the disorders, which should help identify better treatments.

Eating disorders often manifest as a response to a distorted body image that is caused by neurological and biological disorders.

For example, is anorexia the result of skewed body image, self esteem problems, obsessive thoughts, compulsive behavior, or a combination of these? Can it be predicted or identified as a risk factor before drastic weight loss occurs, and therefore avoided?

These and other questions may be answered in the future as scientists and doctors think of eating disorders as medical illnesses with certain biological causes. Researchers are studying behavioral questions, along with genetic and brain systems information, to understand risk factors, identify biological markers and develop medications that can target specific pathways that control eating behavior. Finally, neuroimaging and genetic studies may also provide clues for how each person may respond to specific treatments.

EVALUATING THE AUTHORS' ARGUMENTS:

In the viewpoint you just read, the National Institute of Mental Health suggests that eating disorders are caused by biological and psychological abnormalities in the brain. What pieces of evidence did the authors use to support this claim? Support your answer with material from the text.

Viewpoint 4

Social Factors Contribute to Eating Disorders

Anorexia Nervosa and Related Eating Disorders (ANRED)

"Sometimes appearance-obsessed friends or romantic partners create pressure that encourages eating disorders."

In the following viewpoint ANRED argues that social factors such as friends, family, romantic relationships, peer pressure, and culture contribute to the development of eating disorders. The author explains that just one of these factors might cause disordered eating in one individual, whereas it may take several factors to cause an eating disorder in someone else. Some individuals might develop an eating disorder when facing high expectations from family or friends; others might develop one after observing their mother's unhealthy relationship with food and dieting; still others might develop one as a result of feeling isolated or lonely. Whatever the reason, those vulnerable to eating disorders become obsessed with food as a way to maintain control over stressful or difficult situations. The author concludes that no simple answer addresses the roots of eating disorders, but social pressures likely play a large part.

Anorexia Nervosa and Related Eating Disorders, "What Causes Eating Disorders?" January 1, 2008. Information used with permission of ANRED: Anorexia Nervosa and Related Eating Disorders, Inc. www.anred.com.

Anorexia Nervosa and Related Eating Disorders (ANRED) is a nonprofit organization that provides information about anorexia nervosa, bulimia nervosa, binge-eating disorder, and lesser-known food and weight disorders. Its Web site includes self-help tips and information about recovery and prevention.

AS YOU READ, CONSIDER THE FOLLOWING QUESTIONS:

1. What reason does the author give for daughters of mothers with eating disorders having increased chances of developing an eating disorder themselves?
2. Why does ANRED say that people in danger of developing an eating disorder are often also experiencing relationship problems?
3. What are some of the triggers associated with the onset of an eating disorder, according to ANRED?

There are many theories, many interwoven factors, and no one simple answer that covers a person with an eating disorder. For any particular individual, some or all of the following factors will combine to produce starving, stuffing, and purging. . . .

Family Behavior Can Contribute to an Eating Disorder

Some people with eating disorders say they feel smothered in overprotective families. Others feel abandoned, misunderstood, and alone. Parents who overvalue physical appearance can unwittingly contribute to an eating disorder. So can those who make critical comments, even in jest, about their children's bodies.

Families that include a person with an eating disorder tend to be overprotective, rigid, and ineffective at resolving conflict. Sometimes mothers are emotionally cool while fathers are physically or emotionally absent. At the same time, there are high expectations of achievement and success. Children learn not to disclose doubts, fears, anxieties, and imperfections. Instead they try to solve their problems by manipulating weight and food, trying to achieve the appearance of success even if they do not feel successful.

Research at Oregon Health and Science University in Portland has produced strong evidence that exposure to stress (abuse, neglect, loss of a parent) in childhood increases the risk of behavioral and emotional problems (anxiety, depression, suicidality, drug abuse—phenomena frequently associated with eating disorders) in teenagers and young adults.

Mothers Can Influence Daughters' Body Images

In addition, other research suggests that daughters of mothers with histories of eating disorders may be at higher risk of eating disorders themselves than are children of mothers with few food and weight issues. Children learn attitudes about dieting and their bodies through observation. When mom is dissatisfied with her body and frequently diets, daughters will learn to base their self-worth on their appearance, says Christine Gerbstadt, spokeswoman for the American Dietetic Association.

Alison Field, lead author of a Harvard Study of peer, parent and media influences on children's dieting behavior and body image attutudes, adds that "even small cues—such as making self-deprecating remarks about bulging thighs or squealing in delight over a few lost pounds—can send the message that thinness is to be prized above all else."

According to a report published in the April 1999 issue of the *International Journal of Eating Disorder*, mothers who have anorexia, bulimia, or binge eating disorder handle food issues and weight concerns differently than mothers who have never had eating disorders.

Patterns are observable even in infancy. They include odd feeding schedules, using food for rewards, punishments, comfort, or other non-nutritive purposes, and concerns about their daughters' weight.

Still to be determined is whether or not daughters of mothers with eating disorders will themselves become eating disordered when they reach adolescence.

Restricting Food Can Lead to Disordered Eating

Also, if mothers and fathers preach and nag about junk food and try to limit their children's access to treats, the children will desire and overeat these very items. A recent study indicates that when parents restrict eating, children are more likely to eat when they are not hungry. The more severe the restriction, the stronger the desire to eat prohibited foods. These behaviors may set the stage for a full blown eating disorder in the future.

Relationship Problems Can Contribute to Eating Disorders

Sometimes appearance-obsessed friends or romantic partners create pressure that encourages eating disorders. Ditto for sorority houses, theatre troupes, dance companies, school cliques, and other situations where peers influence one another in unhealthy ways.

People vulnerable to eating disorders, in most cases, are experiencing relationship problems, loneliness in particular. Some may be withdrawn with only superficial or conflicted connections to other people. Others may seem to be living exciting lives filled with friends and social activities, but later they will confess that they did not feel they really fit in, that no one seemed to really understand them, and that they had no true friends or confidants with whom they could share thoughts, feelings, doubts, insecurities, fears, hopes, ambitions, and so forth—the basis of true intimacy. Often they desperately want healthy connections to others but fear criticism and rejection if their perceived flaws and shortcomings become known.

"Unrealistic Cultural Demands" Can Lead to Eating Disorders

In Westernized countries characterized by competitive striving for success, and in pockets of affluence in developing countries, women often experience unrealistic cultural demands for thinness. They respond by linking self-esteem to weight.

Cultural expectations can be cruel and unrelenting. "In order for a woman to consider herself happy, she has to be in a good relationship, be happy with her kids, her friends have to like her, her job has to be going well, her house has to look really good—and she has to be thin." . . .

Major Life Events Can Trigger Eating Disorders

If people are vulnerable to eating disorders, sometimes all it takes to put the ball in motion is a trigger event that they do not know how to handle. A trigger could be something as seemingly innocuous as teasing or as devastating as rape or incest.

Triggers often happen at times of transition, shock, or loss where increased demands are made on people who already are unsure of their ability to meet expectations. Such triggers might include puberty, starting a new school, beginning a new job, death, divorce, marriage, family problems, breakup of an important relationship, critical comments from someone important, graduation into a chaotic, competitive world, and so forth.

> **FAST FACT**
>
> **An Eating Disorder Foundation study found young girls are more afraid of getting fat than of the death of their parents, getting cancer, or facing nuclear war.**

There is some evidence to suggest that girls who achieve sexual maturity ahead of peers, with the associated development of breasts, hips, and other physical signs of womanhood, are at increased risk of becoming eating disordered. They may wrongly interpret their new curves as "being fat" and feel uncomfortable because they no longer look like peers who still have childish bodies.

Wanting to take control and fix things, but not really knowing how, and under the influence of a culture that equates success and happiness with thinness, the person tackles her/his body instead of the problem at hand. Dieting, bingeing, purging, exercising, and other strange behaviors are not random craziness. They are heroic, but misguided and ineffective, attempts to take charge in a world that seems overwhelming.

Sometimes people with medical problems such as diabetes, people who must pay meticulous attention to what they eat, become vulnerable to eating disorders. A certain amount of obsessiveness is necessary for health, but when the fine line is crossed, healthy obsessiveness can quickly become pathological.

Dieting Can Trigger Eating Disorders

Perhaps the most common trigger of disordered eating is dieting. It is a bit simplistic, but nonetheless true, to say that if there were no

Westernized cultural perceptions often equate being overweight with a sense of failure, leading many woman to extreme dieting practices in order to feel loved and successful.

dieting, there would be no anorexia nervosa. Neither would there be the bulimia that people create when they diet, make themselves chronically hungry, overeat in response to hunger pangs and cravings, and then, panicky about weight gain, vomit or otherwise purge to get rid of the calories.

Feeling guilty and perhaps horrified at what they have done, they swear to "be good." That usually means more dieting, which leads to more hunger, and so the cycle repeats again and again. It is axiomatic in eating disorders treatment programs that the best way to avoid a binge is to never, ever allow oneself to become ravenously hungry. It is far wiser to be aware of internal signals and respond to hunger cues early on by eating appropriate amounts of nourishing, healthy food.

EVALUATING THE AUTHORS' ARGUMENTS:

In this viewpoint ANRED claims that dieting can trigger an eating disorder. Do you think that dieting alone is a sufficient explanation for why someone might become eating disordered? Why or why not? Explain your answer thoroughly. Then, list how each author in this chapter might respond to the suggestion that dieting can trigger an eating disorder.

Viewpoint 5

Model Culture Contributes to the Development of Eating Disorders

Emily Nussbaum

"Why are designers casting bodies that are . . . practically indistinguishable from the girls at Renfrew [eating disorder center]?"

In the following viewpoint Emily Nussbaum argues that the modeling industry contributes to the development of eating disorders by holding models to unrealistic weight standards. The majority of models depicted in the media are extremely underweight for their height. Many models take extreme measures to achieve these weights, including becoming anorexic and bulimic, to ensure they find work in the industry. Unfortunately, says Nussbaum, this has proved deadly for a number of models. Despite the deaths and damage to models and women who emulate them, the modeling industry has done little to address the problem. The author concludes that the modeling industry perpetuates eating disorders by sending the dangerous message to young women that to be beautiful, one must be bordering on starvation.

Emily Nussbaum is a writer living in New York. She writes for *Slate, Nerve, Village Voice, New York Times Magazine,* and *Book Review.* She most frequently writes about literature, sexuality, gender, and psychology.

AS YOU READ, CONSIDER THE FOLLOWING QUESTIONS:

1. According to the author, what did model Natalia Vodianova discover about her fellow models when she entered the modeling world at age seventeen?
2. What does the author mean when she says that some models from Eastern Europe find the pressure to be thin a small price to pay?
3. Why do spectators want to see extremely thin models on the runway, in Nussbaum's opinion?

Backstage at the [fashion designer] Carlos Miele show, all the accents are Russian. The models are rubbing off makeup, having transformed from Miele's glamorous jet-setters back into harried teenagers. They look skinny but not cadaverous. Yet after a week in the Bryant Park [New York City public park where Fashion Week is held] tents, I realize I can't trust my own judgment: It's already become impossible to see the difference between thin and thin.

Eating Disorder Debate Affects the Modeling Industry

I walk up to [model] Nataliya Gotsii, who grimaces when I ask her about new industry guidelines on eating disorders. Everyone at Fashion Week makes this face when I raise the subject: After a year of media coverage criticizing the size-zero model, fashion has gotten tired of explaining itself. But Gotsii has particular reason to worry. She was one of the models whose photos have been used to illustrate the controversy—a shot of her ribs was flashed on CNN in order to elicit shocked reactions from celebrities. . . .

A week after our conversation, a perilously thin teenage model, Eliana Ramos, would die in Uruguay, apparently of a heart attack, making it three model deaths in the past seven months. In August, Ramos's older sister Luisel died after restricting herself to a diet of

lettuce leaves and Diet Coke. In November, Brazilian model Ana Carolina Reston died weighing just 88 pounds.

But Gotsii resents being dragged into the debate. In those notorious pictures from last season, she had worn a white halter top dangling from chains; you could count her vertebrae. In a taupe bikini she stood, hands on hips, staring into the camera, a tanned skeleton. . . .

"Eating Was Secondary"

In the great anorexia debate, models are talked about but rarely heard. Which is why it was so startling when Natalia Vodianova, one of those great and silent beautiful ones, the Cinderella from Russia, rose to speak at the Council of Fashion Designers of America panel on eating disorders.

Vodianova stood up, with her sad and enormous eyes, her beautiful wide face familiar from the cover of *Vogue* and ads for Calvin Klein. She began by quoting Oscar Wilde: "'To love oneself is the beginning of a lifelong romance—a very wonderful and inspired saying. But I hope you will agree that no relationship comes that easy.

"I come from a poor background," Vodianova told the carefully vetted crowd of fashionistas and their critics. . . . "I ate because I wanted to stay alive, and it never occurred to me to think of food in any other way." In 2000, when she arrived in Paris at the age of 17, she discovered that her fellow models were obsessed with weight. "At first I kind of sneered, thinking that this would never affect me. But as I began working, I began paying attention to my body shape for the first time. . . . Eating was secondary. But I found a lot of new friends who were living the same lifestyle, and things were far too exciting to worry about it."

At 19, Vodianova gave birth to a son and quickly became skinnier than ever, impressing the fashion world. At five-nine, she weighed only 106 pounds, her hair was thinning, she was anxious and depressed—and she was a runway star with her first major advertising contract. After a friend confronted her, she sought help and got healthier, adding on a few pounds. But when she got up to 112 pounds, her agent sat her down: Designers were complaining she wasn't as thin as she used to be. "I defended myself, saying it was crazy to consider measurements like 33-27-34 to be normal. I think because I was one of the girls most in demand it helped me to be able to forget the incident quickly. On the other hand, it makes me think that if I had been weak at the time, I can really imagine how it could have helped me endanger myself." . . .

FAST FACT

According to the Eating Disorder Foundation, the average American female is 5 feet 4 inches tall and weighs 140 pounds, while the average American female model is 5 feet 11 inches tall and weighs 117 pounds.

Some Models Deny Industry Is Plagued with Eating Disorders

All through Fashion Week, the models told me they felt persecuted by the media conversation, as if they were being blamed for their bodies.

"You know, I don't sing because I don't have the voice," said Flavia, 22, with a sigh. "If I don't have this body, I could not be a model. I eat like a pig!"

"I'm this kind of person who can eat whatever I want," echoed Eva. "I'm so happy that I still can eat ice cream and everything."

"There's always going to be that one somebody who has taken it too far," Sophie told me. I asked her if she knew of anybody who had. No, she said. "All the girls in my model apartment eat everything. We stuff our face."

But another model, Marry Rieder, told me she had no patience for that kind of talk. "It's b.s.," she said flatly on the phone from the Netherlands, where she was busily packing for a photo shoot in Zambia. A Dutch model who has worked to educate the public on the subject of eating disorders, Rieder beat out 20,000 girls to be the face of Guess watches. Then she came to New York, where she was told that if she wanted to do runway work, she needed to lose weight. She dieted and exercised, but that wasn't sufficient.

"I started skipping things. I was still eating, but not enough, really not enough, and going to the gym every day." Her roommates in the model apartment were eating a can of corn a day, Rieder said. "Or an apple. Or whatever. And that's just one of the things I've seen." I asked Rieder if models are open about restricting food. No, she told me. "They hide it. By saying, 'I just ate so much at home, I'm not hungry anymore.' I've heard it a million times."

Why do models not speak out about these issues? "In my opinion, I think it's because they're afraid of losing work," said Rieder.

Models Take Extreme Measures to Be Skinny

Sabrina Hunter, 27, agrees. I found the gorgeous Afro-Caribbean woman not strutting the catwalk but working the Cingular booth in the pavilion outside. She'd left runway modeling, she told me, because the pressure was so intense that it required her to eat in a disordered way. At five-ten, Hunter was expected to be "115 or lower, preferably." After she signed with an American agency, she was given a choice: Lose weight or gain and be a plus-size model. After trying to gain unsuccessfully, she went the opposite direction, eating 600 calories and jogging five miles a day. "It made me extremely moody and depressed. And I looked it, in the face. But that's how all the models look," she says.

Both Rieder and Hunter have known models who are naturally skinny. But many of these girls are exceptionally young: A model who is effortlessly flat-chested and hipless at 14 will start to struggle as she hits her late teens. If she's already rising in the industry, she may find that she needs to take more extreme measures to continue to fit the bony aesthetic. And that goes double for the new breed of models, many of whom come, like Vodianova, from the poorest regions of Eastern Europe. For these girls, pressures to stay thin may be a small price to pay for escaping the small towns they came from. . . .

Models Are Expected to Be Invisible

If Fashion Week is about reinforcing hierarchies, skinniness has always been a way to compete. Being thin means control and, symbolically, that you are rich, that you are young, that you are beautiful, that you

Many models suffer from eating disorders because the fashion industry demands unrealistically thin women and girls to model their clothing. Sisters Luisel and Eliana Ramos, pictured here, both died from heart failure due to extreme thinness.

are powerful. And yet the models themselves, who are skinnier and younger than anyone, seem like the weakest people here: manual laborers with short shelf lives. And whatever their eating habits, the girls in the gowns attract, like anorexics, an unstable mix of envy, anxiety, and scorn, a cultural response reserved for women reduced (or maybe elevated) to their bodies.

And for observers of the catwalk, there remains the nagging question: Why this skinny? Why now? Why are designers casting bodies that are, if not actively anorexic, practically indistinguishable from the girls at Renfrew [an eating disorder treatment center]?

I hear two dominant theories. The first is that fashion is aspirational. There's makeup; there's lighting; it is intended to be extreme, not realistic—to inspire envy, by providing a vision of an impossible life the audience member would love to live. One editor I spoke with wondered if the tiny socialites, the demographic that can afford these expensive garments, naturally prefer to see even tinier girls on the runway, so they could have something to aspire to. According to this theory, we would all love to be that thin.

The other theory is that the girls need to be skinny because they need to be invisible. Clothing stands out best when the body is a blank. And the better the clothes are, the more extreme the skinniness must be. Certainly, the glittering sacks that many designers are featuring these days flatter only a body that recedes inside them (like the [actress] Mary-Kate Olsen look, these puffy garments have an unnerving resemblance to the extra-large sweatshirts I remember anorexics wearing back in college).

But, of course, these two explanations are diametrically opposed. In the first vision, the models must be thin so people look at them. In the second, they must be thin so that no one will notice them. And when I ask the buyers and the customers, they seem baffled about the reason for it all. . . .

The Modeling Industry Sends a Dangerous Message to Young Women

And there are questions it is hard to ask in Fashion World, too bumptious and too basic: Aren't clothes intended to flatter those who purchase them? What kind of message does this send to young women? . . . Isn't there something a little creepy about using teenage girls from poor countries to model gowns that get bought mainly by incredibly wealthy adult women? . . .

Yet despite the jockeying for blame—Are the agents responsible? The magazines? The designers? The stylists?—it's the models who will inevitably be the fall girls, embarrassing the industry when they go one step too far and become thin instead of thin. At times, the issue doesn't seem to be about food at all. It's about the discomfort everyone feels when the girls in the gowns become visible, exposing not just their ribs but the strange vulnerability of their lives.

EVALUATING THE AUTHOR'S ARGUMENTS:

In this viewpoint the author argues that many models develop eating disorders in order to compete in the modeling industry. As a result, many are extremely underweight. What is your opinion about the models you see in advertisements and in magazines? Are they too skinny? What solutions might you suggest for dealing with the problem?

Viewpoint 6

The Internet Contributes to the Development of Eating Disorders

"Countless websites . . . glorify, promote and teach that eating disorders aren't a disease, but a 'lifestyle choice.'"

Kristen Depowski and Kelly Hart

In the following viewpoint Kristen Depowski and Kelly Hart argue that the Internet contributes to the development of eating disorders. They discuss how the Internet has become the best way for adults and teens to learn about eating disorders and use certain sites to teach themselves how to worsen or hide their illness. Currently, the authors explain, there are about five hundred Web sites that teach people how to become anorexic and bulimic. These sites are geared toward young people and promote eating disorders by revealing tips and suggestions for how to lose dangerous amounts of weight. The authors explain that many of these sites also show photos of emaciated models and celebrities as motivation for their members. Depowski and

Kristen Depowski and Kelly Hart, "'Pro-Ana' Web Sites Glorify Eating Disorders: Sites Say Anorexia Isn't a Disease but a Lifestyle Choice," ABCnews.com, June 13, 2006. Reproduced by permission.

Hart conclude that these sites are dangerous because they rationalize and encourage a very serious and potentially deadly disease.

Depowski and Hart are writers for the ABC News Law and Justice Unit.

AS YOU READ, CONSIDER THE FOLLOWING QUESTIONS:

1. According to the authors, what do "pro-ana" and "pro-mia" mean?
2. What about pro-eating-disorder Web sites are particularly attractive to young girls, according to the authors?
3. What tips do the authors provide for recognizing the early signs of an eating disorder?

Bathing suit season is upon us, and more people are hitting the gym and starting new diets trying to shed unwanted pounds. But for millions of Internet-savvy teens, a dangerous alternative is just a click away—countless Web sites that glorify, promote and teach that eating disorders aren't a disease, but a "lifestyle choice." This, despite the fact that eating disorders are one of the most deadly mental illnesses in the country.

Annie Hayashi, spokesperson for the National Association of Anorexia Nervosa and Associated Disorders (ANAD), says that 6 percent of people with eating disorders will eventually die from the disease. "We believe that the pro-eating-disorder sites are not only destructive but dangerous," said Hayashi. "They give legitimacy to people who can't recover and are triggering for people who are trying to recover."

Some Web Sites Glorify Eating Disorders

There are about 500 Web sites that offer tips on how to become anorexic or bulimic. The popularity of what are known as "pro-ana" (pro-anorexia) and "pro-mia" (pro-bulimia) Web sites has increased in recent years. They attract mostly teenage girls and young women, often getting thousands of hits a day.

Most Web sites are run by self-proclaimed "rexies"—individuals who celebrate their eating disorders. Some even call it a religion, reciting psalms and offering prayers to their goddess "Ana." Many of the sites feature "thinspirational" photos, which depict the skin-and-bones of emaciated models and celebrities.

On one site the philosophy is frighteningly blunt: "One day I will be thin enough. Just the bones, no disfiguring flesh. Just the pure clean shape of me, bones. That is what we all are, what we're made up of and everything else is just storage, deposit, waste."

> **FAST FACT**
>
> **According to a 2006 Stanford University study, 50 percent of parents surveyed knew of Web sites that promote eating disorders, 28 percent discussed these sites with their kids, and 20 percent limited their child's Internet use accordingly.**

Most of the Web sites give tips on the most effective way to starve oneself. One site recommends "taking antacids" to "help reduce hunger pains" and constantly drinking coffee, diet soda and chewing gum so "you won't feel hungry." Other tips from similar sites—get manicures to hide your split and broken nails, shower in cold water to burn calories, and wear multiple layers of clothing to hide your weight loss.

Pro-eating-disorder Web Sites Send the Wrong Message

Experts say these so-called "pro-ed" (pro-eating-disorder) Web sites are potentially deadly, particularly because they rationalize and affirm the very behavior that defines the disease. They also package their message in alluring colors, music and designs that attract young girls.

According to Hayashi, "11-, 12-, and 13-year-old girls see and visit these sites and emulate the behavior." She points out that preadolescence is a challenging and confusing time, and teenagers can easily fall prey to the obsessions of this self-destructive and tightly-knit community, resulting in sometimes tragic consequences. "They have an emotional predisposition . . . and are already feeling isolated, with low self-esteem," Hayashi said.

Pro-eating-disorder Web Sites Need to Be Identified

In order to shut down the dangerous Internet forums, Hayashi says ANAD spends a lot of time searching the Internet, identifying pro-eating-disorder sites, then contacting and informing the web servers. Hayashi explains that the only way to get these dangerous sites off the Web is to notify the web servers, which can shut them down for violating the terms and conditions of their Internet agreement.

Another strategy ANAD uses is to report that the various sites contain pornographic images of half-clothed and emaciated young girls, many of whom are underage. While servers such as Yahoo, Lycos and MySpace have been particularly responsive to removing pro-ana and pro-mia Web sites, according to Hayashi, some sites have refused to cooperate with ANAD's requests, citing First Amendment arguments.

Parents' Vigilance Can Protect Teens from Dangerous Web Sites

Advocacy sites like ANAD offer tips for parents to recognize the early-warning signs of eating disorders. Among them: a sudden interest in

Web sites that promote extreme dieting could be contributing to the increase in eating disorders among American teens.

calorie counting, wearing baggy clothing, excessive caffeine consumption, fanatical exercise and a general obsession with weight. These groups urge parents to monitor their children's Internet activity, and keep a watchful eye out for pro-ana and pro-mia sites.

As Hayashi says, parents' vigilance could be a matter of life and death. "The danger of these sites is the sense of community and support they provide. A community some know will mourn them when, not if, they die."

EVALUATING THE AUTHORS' ARGUMENTS:

In this viewpoint the authors describe the ways in which Web sites teach people to become anorexic or bulimic. Because eating disorders are a life-threatening illness, these sites compromise the health and safety of untold numbers of women. In your opinion, how should the problem of pro-eating-disorder Web sites be handled? After you give your opinion, explain how the other authors in this chapter might weigh in on the issue.

Viewpoint 7

Peer Pressure Contributes to Eating Disorders

Hara Estroff Marano

"Perhaps the greatest accelerant of fat fear and distorted eating is the peer culture to which adolescents have been consigned for the past few decades."

In the following viewpoint Hara Estroff Marano argues that eating disorders are often the result of peer pressure. Youth constantly compare themselves to their friends and images they see in the media and pick up on the eating habits of those who surround them. Individuals who engage in disordered eating together often find comfort and even delight in sharing a secret lifestyle. Marano discusses the competition between teens, especially female college students, to obtain the "perfect body." The competition to be thin increases the desire to achieve even greater weight loss. The author concludes that peer pressure can have deadly consequences for those prone to eating disorders. Hara Estroff Marano is the editor at large for *Psychology Today.*

Hara Estroff Marano, "Skinny Sweepstakes," *Psychology Today,* April 2, 2008.

AS YOU READ, CONSIDER THE FOLLOWING QUESTIONS:

1. According to the viewpoint, why does the college environment lend itself to the development of eating disorders?
2. What is the strongest predictor of eating disorders among middle-school girls today, according to a report in the *International Journal of Eating Disorders?*
3. What percent of females experience an eating disorder at some point during their college years?

"I started starving myself when I was 12 or 13," Chloe, an absolute beauty, recalls. "I wasn't overweight, but I wasn't as thin as a lot of my friends. It was just something I noticed."

Around that time, "a lot of problems" erupted in her family. "Dieting made me feel like I was in control of something. It was the one thing I knew I could change on my own. I would diet and get positive feedback and feel really good. So I wouldn't eat for a few days at a time."

Dieting also bound her to her peers. "A lot of girls at school would skip meals. We'd do it together. We went on fad diets together, too." Her family never noticed her food fetishes. "I had trouble impressing my mother. I could never achieve enough for her. But she definitely noticed when I lost weight."

From the beginning, starving consumed her life. "You think about it everywhere you go. And you compare yourself to other people. Each of my friends was vying to be better than the others. I was in a restaurant with my boyfriend and a girl walked in who was really pretty and much thinner than me. I saw him glance at her. I went into the bathroom and cried."

She couldn't look at a picture of a celebrity without feeling bad, either. The boys at her public school didn't help. "They're constantly comparing women to each other: 'That girl is really hot; she's so much hotter than her friends.' So we compete to be the hotter friend. Some days it makes you feel fat. On particularly bad days, I can look at children and think that when I'm older, that little 3-year-old girl is going to steal my husband."

The Quest for the Perfect Body

In a culture of plenty where the young are pressured to succeed even before birth, the achievement package has come to include, especially for girls, a "perfect" body. Starting at puberty, sometimes before, the mounting pressure launches girls into the stratosphere of fat fear, in part fueled by the ubiquity of food, in part by new sensitivities adolescence brings to the judgments of others.

But perhaps the greatest accelerant of fat fear and distorted eating is the peer culture to which adolescents have been consigned for the past few decades. Age segregation isn't new to America's schools. But since the middle of the 20th century, it has gathered critical mass until it has also come to dominate the extracurricular life of the young in their insular march through middle school, high school, and beyond.

Between 1960 and 2000, the percentages of 20-, 25-, and 30-year-olds enrolled in school more than doubled, with females becoming an increasingly larger part of the total.

The extension of schooling for more young people, especially girls—now the majority of college attendees—requires them to be warehoused together for years with those deliberately selected to share many of the same attributes, constraining exposure to the broader range of humanity. Ongoing shifts in communication technology (think: MySpace, YouTube, and mp3 files) may employ up-to-the-nanosecond science, but they turn out to be extraordinarily conservative social and developmental forces, keeping the young tightly tethered to each other, cloistered among those like themselves, and sharing sights, sounds, and other cultural effusions targeted exclusively at them, further age-stratifying their souls.

Superimpose on that nature's compulsory contribution, the mating sweepstakes, and each cohort of girls seems forced to make ever more minute distinctions between themselves—just as they compete to distinguish themselves on their college application essays. Thus does dieting become a competitive sport with the gold medal going to the thinnest, a triumph of the cultural ideal for appearance that almost every American girl will unwittingly internalize by middle school.

The strongest predictor of eating disorders among middle-school girls today is the importance that peers place on weight and eating, researchers report in the *International Journal of Eating Disorders.* The perceptions of peers outweighs, as it were, such traditional factors as confidence level, actual body mass, trying to look like the girls and women appearing on television and in magazines, even being teased by family and others about weight.

In highly age-stratified education, particularly for females, whose attractiveness depends so heavily on youth, "all the most attractive females of a cohort are competing with each other" for the attention of males, explains Geoffrey Miller. "They are seeing only rivals who are quite similar to themselves," says the University of New Mexico psychologist. "They're not seeing the mating market as a whole. Their frame of reference is artificially constricted."

The result is "extreme intensification of sexual competition." And with increasing numbers of young women not merely going to college but getting advanced degrees, age segregation and stratification continue much later in life than they did even a few decades ago.

Modern schools, Miller points out, are often so homogenous in terms of class and race as well as age that "kids have to invent ways to be different from each other that they never would have had to invent a hundred years ago." As they jockey intensely for skinny status, their very limited involvement with the outside world helps keep them highly focused on themselves.

Adrift Amid Peer Pressure

Richard Hersh calls it the culture of neglect: kids grow up overly dependent on their peers—"in essence, kids raising kids"—without developing a strong sense of self. A RAND scholar, former director of Harvard's Center for Moral Education, as well as former president of Trinity College and William Smith and Hobart Colleges, Hersh contends that adults—parents, neighbors, teachers, professors—have inadvertently done children and adolescents an injustice. They allow them to be socialized by television, the Internet, and by their peers rather than by caring, demanding, and mentoring adults. At the same time, the adults view kids as helpless, sheltering them from a wide range of experiences, "the risk of failure and being hurt being so great."

Both forms of deprivation weaken the young from within, so that kids go off to college socially and emotionally fragile, manifest in a rising tide of distress: anorexia and bulimia, along with depression, physical violence, alcohol and other drug abuse, and suicide attempts.

Eating Disorders Hit Home in the United States

Forty-two percent of Americans–about four out of ten–either have suffered or have known someone who has suffered from an eating disorder.

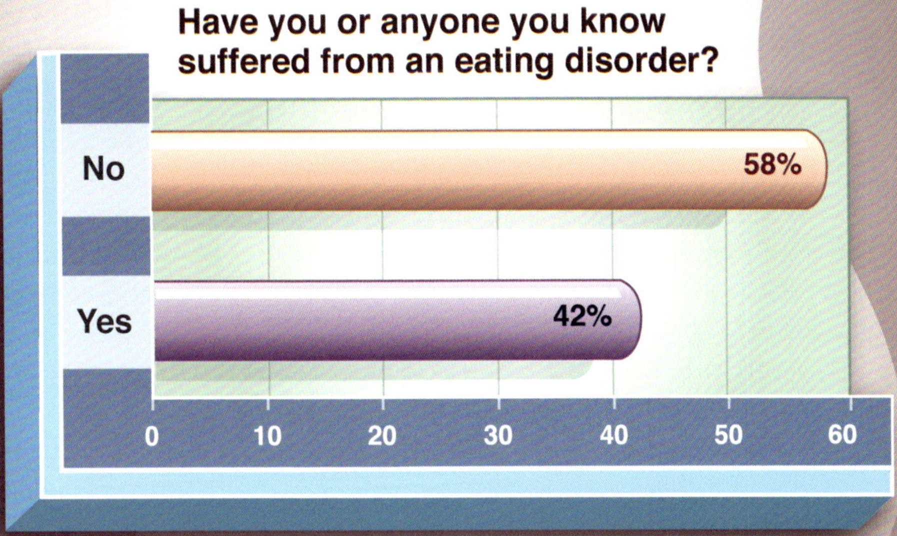

Taken from: National Eating Disorders Association (NEDA) and GMI, Inc., 2005.

Approximately 40 percent of females now experience an eating disorder at some point during their years of college, data show.

Missing in action is a rich internal life independent of peers. Hersh sees residential college life perpetuating and intensifying an adolescent pattern of overreliance on peer approval. It also, he says, elevates the body over the mind. And that combination subverts the developmental challenge of finding something far more durable: a stable identity.

The way New York psychotherapist Steven Levenkron sees it, the adults essentially outsource parenting. Levenkron has been treating young women with eating disorders for more than 30 years. He wrote one of the first books about anorexia, *The Best Little Girl in the World*, in 1978, and he has written textbooks on treatment of the disorder. Why is it, he asks, that some girls succumb to the peer pressure and some don't? "Those who aren't mentored by parents are not inoculated against peer pressure. They wind up turning to their peers and to the media, to the outside society, for guidance on how to appeal to men." Without a strong, healthy attachment to parents, kids become fair game for what he sees as destructive messages about femininity from Hollywood.

But the damage goes especially deep because contemporary adolescents "have no language for reflection," he says. "They don't know how to think about hurts. That makes them feel alone in the world." Anorexics, he contends, have only a very primitive language. "They can talk your head off about body measurements and fats. It's all transacted with about 12 words."

From Comparison to Cutthroat Competition

It's bad enough that teens are swaddled in software and bound by a branch of consumer culture crafted exclusively for them. But there is something about herding them together 24/7 that actively distorts their thinking, specifically about bodies. As a result, America's universities have become incubators of eating disorders. Attending a residential college actually warps perception of self in relation to others, finds psychologist Catherine Sanderson. At a time and place where people should be getting smarter about everything, they are getting a lot less smart about themselves.

Fast Fact

Research by Debbie Franko, professor of counseling and applied psychology at Northeastern University, found that girls who engage in "diet talk" with other girls for long periods of time are more likely to develop an eating disorder.

Mistakenly, they assume that other people's statements accurately reflect their behavior. They know that they themselves talk the talk in the dining hall and other public places—but privately slip out later for a bag of Doritos. They feel ashamed and isolated, without realizing that almost everyone else is wolfing down chips in private, too. Students develop a false impression of the norm.

But the damage is done. The feelings of shame and isolation lead almost directly to bingeing and purging and other forms of disordered eating. "The more women perceive themselves as different, the more symptoms they show of anorexia or bulimia," Sanderson finds.

"The problem with college is that the norms are in your face," she notes. You eat in a common dining hall, exercise in a common fitness center, shower together, and get dressed together. "The togetherness surrounds people at the key life period in which this stuff matters."

Norms matter especially at times of transition, such as going off to boarding school or starting college. In order to make it in their new environment, students look to others there to figure out what's normal. We all navigate the social universe by making comparisons to others, but researchers have long known that widespread insecurity (Will I get into Harvard? Is my family coming apart at the seams? Do I even have an identity of my own? Why do I feel so different from everyone?) exacerbates the process, turning comparison—with peers, with media figures—into cutthroat competition.

In such environments, misperception accelerates over time. Asked what they weigh, freshmen say "around 130," exactly what they believe other women weigh. But surveyed again the next year, after gaining about five pounds, the same women say—accurately—that they weigh 135. However, they think others weigh "around 125." "You're gaining weight and you know it, yet you believe that other women are losing weight," explains Sanderson. It's ironic, she notes, that this is a topic about which college actually makes people stupid: The more time they spend in school, the less accurate they become in their perceptions.

Puppets of Fear

Columbia University psychologist Barbara Von Bulow co-runs a day-treatment program in Manhattan for eating disordered students who have been sent home on leave, asked by their out-of-town colleges to take time off for treatment. So competitive are the women about their weight-control strategies that the program has had to separate the bulimics from the anorexics.

"It's difficult to treat anorexics if they don't see themselves as unhealthy," Von Bulow observes. "Yet the bulimics look at the anorexics as successes because they are so thin." On the other hand, the anorexics "are terrified when they look at the bulimics, most of whom are normal weight. They see them as failed anorexics."

Extremely thin celebrities such as Calista Flockhart (pictured center, with the cast of the television show Ally McBeal*) can add to the peer pressure girls and women feel to achieve similar body types.*

In reality, as in the dictionary, anorexia comes before bulimia; about 50 percent of the time, restrictive eating begets binge eating. Candice Sombrero, 19, a sophomore at Babson College outside Boston, endured six months of anorexia while a student at the prestigious Iolani School in Honolulu, where she grew up. "I'd grab coffee at home and tell my parents I'd get breakfast at school, which I never did. For lunch I prided myself on sipping an extra-large Diet Coke." The endless hunger made her preoccupied with food. "Once you get your hands on food, you stuff yourself. Then you feel physically uncomfortable and guilty for eating, so you start to purge." For the next year and a half, she was "stuck in the bulimic cycle, throwing up eight to 10 times a day."

Bulimia testifies to the difficulty of the restrictive eating that defines anorexia. On the other hand, not every girl can make herself throw up. Katy Palmer is one of the latter.

At 17, she was at the top of her high school class in Atlanta, looking at colleges and locked into competition with another girl for class valedictorian. "We knew each other's GPA down to the hundredth of a point," she recalls. The academic pressure was intense. That year her grandfather died, and suddenly family life was dominated by grieving. "I didn't have control over the college application process and I couldn't make any school accept me; I knew it was an arbitrary process. I didn't have control over what was happening in my family. Eating became the least complicated thing I could do that was under my control. I read an article in *Self* magazine all about calories. Cause and effect were clear: Fewer calories equal less weight."

Gradually, she shriveled into her five-foot-10-inch frame, until she weighed 115 pounds. "I was always in a bad mood. I stopped having a personality. I stopped thinking about boys. All I thought about was food. Everything had to be carefully portioned. Any spread of food, any open box, was dangerous waters. I was always hungry. My dreams were nightmares about eating too much."

But people told her she looked great. And her parents never picked up on her calorie restriction. In fact, she became locked into competition with her mother, a true peer in weight obsession. "She'd say, 'Your thighs are skinnier than mine; let's get out the tape measure.' We never actually did, but we did feed off each other. We talked about how good it feels to be hungry. She told me she wouldn't be attracted to my father if he were overweight.

"Initially it's a choice," she says now. "You start dieting to be in control. But then it veers out of control. Anorexia is so dictated by fear. You're just a puppet of fear." That sleight of slight is likely accomplished through an array of cognitive changes, purely the effects of starvation on the brain.

Perfect on Paper

Fear is the dark heart of contemporary girl culture. Courtney Martin, an instructor at Barnard College and author of *Perfect Girls, Starving Daughters: The Frightening New Normalcy of Hating Your Body*, contends that a whole generation of young women was told that they could be anything. What they heard was slightly different: "We have to be everything." And that's terrifying. The pre-college emphasis on achievement leads them "to compose the self as perfect, with a perfect resume and a perfect body," since they were socialized to believe they can look any way they want if they just try hard enough. Unfortunately, it's hard to create a sustainable self-image without a sense of self.

The pursuit of perfection is always self-consuming, and it locks young women into a vicious cycle. The struggle to achieve so much in so many different areas overwhelms them with anxiety, and anxiety generates constant comparison, which only makes them see themselves more negatively, which pressures them to try harder.

Martin regards the rising rate of suicide among girls 10 to 14 as alarming proof that girls today increasingly lack the inner resources to disarm the anxiety of achievement pressure and fat fear. "Neither parents nor schools are nurturing kids' well-being," she says, "because they themselves are caught up in the anxiety dance."

Psychologist Janell Mensinger views it as fallout of the Superwoman Syndrome. Head of health research at Reading Hospital in Pennsylvania, Mensinger has been looking at eating disorders among girls for over a decade. In a recent study reported in the journal *Sex Roles*, she and her colleagues found that the more adolescent girls perceived behavioral commands for excellence in academics, appearance, and dating, the more they subscribed to the superwoman ideal and the more disordered their eating became.

What's more, in surveying 1,200 students in 11 schools in New York City and Philadelphia, she found that the all-girls schools fostered greater competitiveness on appearance-related issues than did the coed schools. "Girls at single-sex schools appear to be at a disadvantage in that they are more dissatisfied with their bodies," she reports.

That body competition is worse among students at all-girls schools makes perfect sense to Geoffrey Miller. The psyche reads the environment as a scarcity of males. And that only ups the mate competition among females. "It's a supply-and-demand effect," he suggests. Candice Sombrero would agree. A transfer student, she finds that eating disorders are much less prevalent at Babson than at most other schools. "This is a business college, and the ratio of males to females is 60:40 or 70:30."

If it is indeed a supply-and-demand effect, then America's campuses ought to be bracing for a near epidemic of eating disorders. The ratio of males to females is shrinking dramatically at most colleges; even Babson, able to draw from a larger pool of women, aims to add more female students.

It is a particularly cruel irony that, through unforeseen shifts in gender balance, higher education as it's now constituted winds up lowering the threshold for one of the most mentally and physically disabling disorders of our time.

Pressure Control

Just as there is no single cause of eating disorders among the young—they are rooted in conditions set long before college—there is no one solution. But many contributing elements can be addressed by schools, parents, and the culture at large.

- Attenuate the competitive pressure on kids; dispute the idea that the only path to success runs through Harvard Yard.
- Combat the pursuit of perfection: Discuss the impossibility of being perfect, the self-preoccupation that dogs perfectionists, and perfectionism's ultimately self-defeating nature.
- Allow the young meaningful engagement in a broad range of experiences beyond their usual routines.
- Encourage kids to experiment by giving them permission to fail, so they can claim their own experience and construct a strong sense of self.
- Discard helicopter parenting for real parenting, because authentic connection inoculates kids against the excesses of peer culture.
- Expose kids to alternatives to the pseudo culture mass manufactured for their consumption.
- Lobby upper schools to dampen the college-entrance sweepstakes. This in turn could force colleges to revamp admissions policies predicated on excess selectivity favoring ultracompetitive overachievers.

EVALUATING THE AUTHOR'S ARGUMENTS:

In the viewpoint you just read, the author quotes individuals who have struggled with an eating disorder who describe how it was triggered by peer pressure. The author also uses results from studies and information from scholars to back up her viewpoint. Does a personal story have as much validity as someone who writes on the subject without having experience with an eating disorder? Explain your reasoning.

Chapter 3

How Should Web Sites That Promote Eating Disorders Be Viewed?

Women who suffer from eating disorders often turn to online communities that promote anorexia and bulimia, which help them feel less lonely and isolated.

Viewpoint 1

Pro-eating-disorder Web Sites Should Be Shut Down

Jill Meredith Collins

"Many personal web page servers . . . have banned pro-anorexic sites on the domains which they sponsor."

In the following viewpoint Jill Meredith Collins argues that pro-eating-disorder Web sites disseminate dangerous information and should be shut down. Hundreds of these sites exist on the Internet, where they provide a forum for people to discuss their experiences. While many of these sites operate under the pretense that they provide a supportive, educational environment, they often do little more than fuel an individual's desire to remain eating disordered, the author states. Furthermore, says Collins, the members experience a false sense of camaraderie with other members. This is dangerous because it negatively reinforces an unhealthy behavior and reduces the likelihood that an individual will seek help or work on recovery. Collins concludes the only way to combat the deadly influence of pro-eating-disorder Web sites is to shut them down altogether.

Jill Meredith Collins, "Nurturing Destruction: Eating Disorders Online," *off our backs*, vol. 34, pp. 20–22.

Collins is a contributor to *off our backs*, a feminist magazine that provides news and information about women's lives and feminist activism.

AS YOU READ, CONSIDER THE FOLLOWING QUESTIONS:

1. What kind of content does the author say is found on pro-eating-disorder Web sites?
2. What does the author mean when she says that pro-eating-disorder Web sites often reinforce a person's eating disorder rather than provide help?
3. According to the author, what seems to be the main purpose of pro-eating-disorder Web sites?

It's a typical day for an adolescent female. She wakes up and notices whether or not she's hungry, eats a light, fat-free breakfast if she thinks she's too hungry to make it until lunch, which she'll probably skip so she can eat a full dinner so as not to worry her parents. She is surrounded by images of thin women, and she knows that all women don't look like [singer] Christina Aguilera, but her subconscious registers her own body type as being something other than beautiful. If her jeans fit a little more tightly than they did the day before, she feels like crying. If she manages to shed a few pounds, she'll be praised for it by peers and even adults. The teen magazines that she looks to for guidance warn her of eating disorders, but they show pictures of girls who are little more than skeletons, while the opposite page shows a 100-pound model who could just as easily be undernourished. She knows the danger, and yet she wonders, how hard it would it be to just let it happen? Be skinny, be praiseworthy, get attention . . . even if that attention ends up being medical attention. . . .

Hundreds of Pro-eating-disorders Web Sites Exist

It is because of my memories of life in the impressionable pre-anorexic mind that I worry about the generation of girls growing up after me.[1] The images of females in the media haven't changed since then. In

1. The author suffered with anorexia as an adolescent.

fact, probably the only major change in the media in the past ten years has been the rise of Internet usage. And this combination of factors has resulted in a very disturbing trend: pro-anorexia Web sites. Or, as the sites like to call themselves, "pro-ana." When they refer to bulimia, then it's "mia." Eating disorders in general are simply shortened to "eds." Another word that has been coined for this phenomenon is "thinspiration," which usually involves pictures of extremely thin women, both models and clinically thin victims of anorexia.

The Eating Disorders Association believes at least 400 pro-anorexia sites and chatrooms currently exist on the Internet. The content of the sites usually consists of online journaling about anorexic behaviors and comments on the journaling. Girls exchange tips on how to perpetuate the disorder and how to hide it from others. The most popular tagline is "Anorexia is a lifestyle, not a disease."

The sites generally operate under the pretense of support, and some of them may actually accomplish that for girls who are already anorexic and do not intend to recover. The question is whether support for their state is actually a good thing. Some of the contributors say they "suffer" from "ana," while others relish it and say they enjoy it. They refuse help in getting better. But very few eating disorder victims are willing to go into recovery until someone intervenes and insists on it (in my case, it was my mother). Some of the sites want to help minimize the damage to the body; others are overtly harmful. They naively believe that their words do not influence others, but I have read the following sentence on an online diary: "I think I might cut up my gums so it hurts to eat so I won't want to; I saw that on a pro-ana site." This statement is proof of at least one instance where the sites have been used as instructional.

FAST FACT

After several pleas from the organization Anorexia Nervosa and Associated Disorders, Yahoo! removed 115 pro-ana Web sites.

Pro-anorexia Web Sites Do Not Help

Many other anorexic girls, however, wander into these "anorexic communities" looking for support in conquering something that is on the verge of destroying them. They do not get the help they need from the

Message in a Web Site

A 2006 review of pro-anorexia Web sites found they pushed ideas of perfection, isolation, control, and deceit, among others.

Prevalent Themes Extracted from the Pro-ana Web Sites

Theme	Description
Control	Web sites alleged that successful weight loss helps control a person's body and life.
Success	Success was associated with strength and measured by weight loss. Only those who are strong can lose weight successfully and keep the weight off.
Perfection	Society and cultural "norms" equate thinness with perfection and support its pursuit.
Isolation	People with eating disorders are alone. Befriending the eating disorder leads to isolation from others.
Sacrifice	Foregoing friends, school, family, and relationships are necessary to foster continued success with the eating disorder. The Web sites encourage this sacrifice.
Transformation	Eating disorders can transform a person from being "fat and ugly" to being "thin and beautiful." The transformation is fostered by successful and continued weight loss.
Coping	Eating disorders are a means of coping with difficult life situations (abuse, troubled relationships, death) and problematic feelings (sadness, loneliness). The Web sites offer a way to cope or manage the eating disorder as opposed to "treating" the eating disorder.
Deceit	Individuals may have to deceive others to protect their eating disorder. Hiding weight loss and abnormal eating attitudes and behaviors is necessary to prevent discovery of the eating disorder.
Solidarity	These Web sites allow people with eating disorders to survive in a world that views the eating disorders community as tragic, dangerous, and disgraceful. The Web sites are a place where the eating disorder community can remain strong and supportive of one another.
Revolution	Individuals with anorexia nervosa should channel their strengths into other areas of life that require reform.

Taken from: Mark L. Norris, et al., "Ana and the Internet: A Review of Pro-anorexia Websites," *International Journal of Eating Disorders*, vol. 39, no. 6, September 2006, p. 446.

pro-anorexia Web sites; instead they get reinforcement of the problem that they want to overcome. In that stage, it's very difficult to overcome something when others are convincing you that you don't need to. I remember the "you've lost weight" compliments when I was very sick, and how they made me struggle with whether to recover at all. I always told myself that the givers of these compliments had no idea what they were saying because they did not know I was anorexic. These memories convince me that someone knowing you were anorexic, and still reinforcing it, could easily drive a young girl over the edge.

A number of "pro-ana" communities exist on the popular LiveJournal.com server. One such community states on its profile, "This is a supportive community for anorexics and bulimics. This is not a debate community and there will be no bashing of our views. This community is especially created for thinspiration such as thinspiring pictures or poems or stories. All are welcome." The comment on bashing of their views seems to be echoed in the profile of another community:

> "If you are anti-ed, then you are NOT welcome here. How about you all stop treating people with eds like little children who don't know any better? We know the health side effects because we live with them everyday [sic]. I think it's cruel that you all make jokes at people with eating disorder's expense and then try to justify it by saying you just want them to be happy and eat healthy. You just want someone to attack and belittle is what your problem is. I don't want to hear about society. What else do you morons ever say? And quit stalking ed related communities. Some people are happy at their weight but we are not. So go away. Don't bother to join this community and post [expletive] because I'll delete and remove you faster than you can wipe your [expletive]. . . .

The fatality factor seems to be ignored by these sites. I have even seen one that was "in memory of __________ who died of anorexia. She was an avid pro-anorexic." The logic in that baffles me. When someone dies of AIDS, we don't try to help AIDS patients stay sick. What would we say if people with heart disease had online communities where they egged each other on in eating Big Macs? One member of a pro-anorexia forum offers "fasting" tips, then wraps them up by saying, "BUT MOST IMPORTANT: If you die, all your hard work is USELESS. So don't die, ok? Cause I'll miss you!"

Many online pro-eating-disorder communities use images of models or very thin celebrities to support their ideas that being thin means being beautiful.

Pro-eating-disorder Web Sites Should Be Banned

Many personal web page servers, such as Angelfire and Yahoo, have banned pro-anorexic sites on the domains which they sponsor. The majority of the pro-anorexic sites that thrive are on online diary services such as Live Journal and Diaryland. Many people suspect that the Web sites exist for shock value and attention-getting, which is a viable theory considering the overtly rough language and seemingly ignorant stance of the "pro-ana" sites.

Naturally, pro-anorexia sites catch the eyes of many concerned individuals such as myself. I have been brave enough to approach the sites with comments along the lines of "please understand that anorexia is a serious disease. I suffered it myself, and I strongly encourage you to get help. Please think about the effect that your Web site could have on people." Most of these comments go ignored, not suprisingly. . . .

It terrifies me to think about what would have happened if I had seen these sites just a few short years ago. I am saddened and disgusted that the consciousness of our culture has led not only to breeding eating disorders in young girls, but now in allowing them to purposely nurture one another's harmful behavior. These are our young girls, and this is the world they are growing up in. They believe themselves to be adults beyond a need for guidance—but who among us remembers being fifteen and impressionable? Who among us is glad that our distorted self-destructive notions were not encouraged any further than they were? Who among us is glad to still be here today, having won (or almost won) the battles we fought as a teenager? Maybe sites like these will always exist, but shouldn't we at least be making the effort to outweigh them with nurturing of another kind?

EVALUATING THE AUTHORS' ARGUMENTS:

In this viewpoint Collins argues that the only way to protect adolescents from pro-eating-disorder Web sites is to shut them down. How do you think the author of the following viewpoint, Gracie Doran, might respond to this argument? Explain your answer using evidence from the texts.

Viewpoint 2

Pro-eating-disorder Web Sites Are Detrimental but Have a Right to Exist

"We cannot choose what can be put on the Internet and what can't."

Gracie Doran

In the following viewpoint Gracie Doran argues against shutting down pro-eating-disorder Web sites. The author argues that although some of these sites contain harmful content, the people behind the sites are protected by their right to free speech. In the author's opinion, free speech should be protected at all costs, as it is un-American to censor people. In addition, the author argues that many pro-eating-disorder sites put disclaimers and warnings up to dissuade anyone vulnerable to eating disorders from looking at them. Finally, Doran argues it is ultimately the user's responsibility to decide what content to view online. She concludes that although not everyone agrees with everything they read and hear, these Web sites have just as much of a right to exist as any other site on the Internet.

Gracie Doran, "Everything Online Should Not Be Digested," *Daily Evergreen*, July 13, 2006. Reproduced by permission.

Doran was a sophomore when she wrote this article for the *Daily Evergreen,* a student-run newspaper at Washington State University.

AS YOU READ, CONSIDER THE FOLLOWING QUESTIONS:

1. According to the author, pro-eating-disorder Web sites offer a place for what?
2. What connection does the author make between pro-eating-disorder Web sites and pornography Web sites?
3. What does the author mean when she says, "Free speech is a good and necessary part of our society"?

Need tips for choosing the right classes? How about help with what to wear for a job interview? What about where you should stay on vacation? How about being anorexic?

Information About Eating Disorders Can Be Found Online

With the Internet creating a worldwide network, anyone can get virtually any information they want. However, easy availability also brings access to materials that aren't very good for society.

Pornographic materials are available online, along with instructions for making methamphetamines, constructing a bomb and other dangerous or illicit information. One of the newer trends in Web sites is about eating disorders: Not just giving information about them, but also supporting them as a life choice.

Anorexia and bulimia support groups are now only a click away. Pro-ana (short for anorexia) is a social movement that promotes the view of anorexia as a lifestyle, instead of a disorder. These sites include discussion forums, "thinspiration" pictures and quotes, and poetry to advocate the lifestyle idea. It is a place for self-identified people with eating disorders to come together.

Pro-eating-disorder Web Sites Offer Advice

So far this notion doesn't seem as disgusting as other materials online do, but hold that thought.

Cartoon by Dan Rosandich. www.CartoonStock.com.

These Web sites offer advice on how to live with an eating disorder and embrace it. The people—usually women—in the discussion groups talk about Ana (anorexia) and Mia (bulimia) as if they are real people.

The sites feature letters from Ana and Mia that include statements like: "You fat cow you deserve to be in pain," and "I shall tell you a secret now: Deep down inside themselves, they are disappointed with you. Their daughter, the one with so much potential, has turned into a fat, lazy and undeserving girl."

The eating disorder takes on a character—almost like a controlling companion. However, this companion enjoys hurting and destroying its acquaintances.

Warnings Appear on Pro-eating-disorder Web Sites

Yes, many of these sites do have an entrance page letting the viewer know the site isn't for people who don't have eating disorders or aren't viewing the condition as a life choice. They also say eating disorders can be life threatening.

However this useless, so-called precaution is similar to that of other Web sites containing questionable content. Pornographic sites have a Web page upon arrival, asking you to verify that you are over 18. Yet, a 15-year-old could view the inappropriate content just as easily. The same goes for Web sites geared toward helping people with eating disorders continue to malnourish themselves and for others to begin.

According to ABC News, Annie Hayashi, spokeswoman for the National Association of Anorexia Nervosa and Associated Disorders, said, "We believe that the pro-eating-disorder sites are not only destructive but dangerous. They give legitimacy to people who can't recover and are triggering for people who are trying to recover."

Many pro-ana sites do address this issue upon arrival at the page; saying to choose not to view the page is a matter of self-control. Yet anorexia is a disease comparable to addiction, in which self-control is not always easy.

These sites dispute that anorexia and bulimia are diseases, portraying them instead as philosophies of life. They offer tips on how to lose weight, including vomiting as well as other methods, and how to hide eating disorders from family members or friends. Among these tips are: "If you have hunger pains, hit yourself in the stomach" or "Pinch your thigh to know that you don't need to eat." People adding to the forums seem to celebrate their eating disorder.

FAST FACT

The British mental health charity SANE found that 97 percent of pro-ana visitors are women between the ages of thirteen and forty-nine. Almost half the respondents said they visited a pro-ana site several times a day.

Pro-eating-disorder Web Sites Are Protected by Free Speech

How can sites such as these be allowed? Unfortunately, we cannot choose what can be put on the Internet and what can't. Free speech is a good and necessary part of our society. However, one must think about the potential damage sites like these can cause to young girls and boys viewing this content.

Even though some Web sites offer extreme dieting tips which can encourage people to develop an eating disorder, their content is protected by free speech.

The issue here is that the people who support pro-eating-disorder Web sites are wrongly justifying their disease and whether intentionally or not, are influencing people to join them. The Internet is like most things used to convey information—good and bad information can find its way to the user. However, the information can be obtained much easier on the Internet and this is what sets it apart from other sources. Right or wrong, this information is out there. Be aware that, like most things, not everything you find on the Internet should be taken with you.

EVALUATING THE AUTHOR'S ARGUMENTS:

In this viewpoint the author argues that pro-eating-disorder Web sites are protected by free speech and cannot be shut down. Do you agree that Web sites with potentially dangerous content should be protected by free speech? Why or why not?

Viewpoint 3

Pro-eating-disorder Web Sites Are Dangerous

Natasha Courtenay-Smith

"Pro-anorexia Web sites are condemned by doctors who say they actively encourage mental illness."

In the following viewpoint Natasha Courtenay-Smith argues that Web sites that promote eating disorders are extremely dangerous. She describes hundreds of Web sites that encourage disordered eating, saying they are usually run by young women who suffer from eating disorders themselves. While some of these sites claim to help those with eating disorders, many sites actually glorify and idolize thin celebrities, offer advice on how to conceal eating disordered behaviors, and applaud member weight loss. Courtenay-Smith worries that these sites create a cult-like mentality that threatens the health of adolescents who are particularly vulnerable to peer pressure and provocative suggestions about weight and body image. The author concludes that these sites are dangerous because they worsen the problem of eating disorders.

Courtenay-Smith is a journalist whose work has appeared in the *Independent,* the

Natasha Courtenay-Smith, "The Cult of Anorexia," *Daily Mail* (UK), June 29, 2006.

Sunday Telegraph, and the *Financial Times Magazine*. She is also a regular contributor to the *Daily Mail*, Britain's second largest daily newspaper.

AS YOU READ, CONSIDER THE FOLLOWING QUESTIONS:

1. Who is Marjorie Wallace, and what is her opinion of pro-eating-disorder sites?
2. What does the word *macabre* mean in the context of the viewpoint?
3. What health problems do anorexic women develop, as reported by Courtenay-Smith?

Lavinia Walker has anorexia. Her weight occupies her every waking thought, and her willpower is such that she can survive on a daily diet of a handful of cornflakes and a single rich tea biscuit without feeling hunger.

The severity of her illness is such that she has even tried to perform liposuction on herself, resulting in angry scars across her abdomen. Hers is an extreme position, but not one that she is duly concerned about. Lavinia has had anorexia before, but has entered into this latest episode with some determination.

Lavinia, 24, is a member of the pro-anorexia movement, nicknamed 'pro-ana' by its members, currently experiencing an alarming online revival. Comprised of numerous unregulated groups, many of which are thought to be run from the bedrooms of young women suffering from eating disorders, the members see anorexia as a 'lifestyle choice' and not a disease.

Pro-ana Sites Idolize Thin Celebrities

Yesterday, the [*Daily*] *Mail* reported an alarming link between these so-called pro-ana sites and extremely slender celebrities. [Singer] Victoria Beckham, in particular, is cited by users of the sites as being the star they would most like to look like. "I envy her thin legs and chest," wrote one woman. "She has beautiful bones sticking out of her chest."

On another such site, one girl commented: "Posh [Beckham's nickname] is a major hottie! I love her arms! If I could look like her, I would never have a problem with anything."

Marjorie Wallace, chief executive of mental health charity Sane, said: "There is an element of worship of the thin, and that is where bringing celebrities into it can be so dangerous. These Web sites integrate pictures of beautiful celebrities with other pictures showing ravaged sufferers of eating disorders, and it reinforces the belief that it is an achievement to be thin." . . .

Doctors Shun Pro-eating-disorder Web Sites

Despite a cull of pro-anorexia Web sites by Internet service providers in 2001 following a public outcry, the movement is continuing to thrive. Drawn to the Internet's shroud of anonymity, anorexic girls support one another in their chosen method of losing weight.

In macabre chat rooms they peruse images of skeletal bodies, applaud weight loss and offer advice on everything from how to resist hunger cravings to how to fool your family into thinking you are eating.

Lavinia, who logs on to pro-anorexia Web sites for inspiration and support, is a fierce defender of the movement. She says it has helped keep her alive as well as providing her with information about how to starve herself 'safely'. It is, however, difficult to entirely comprehend her views when, not only is her own ill-health immediately apparent, but a quick glance at various pro-ana sites yields troubling advice about such things as how to make yourself be sick.

Certainly, pro-anorexia Web sites are condemned by doctors who say they actively encourage a mental illness which already affects almost half a million people in the UK. Medical professionals also suggest the sites have helped spawn a generation of anorexic girls who enjoy their plight and as such have no wish to recover.

"Thinspiration" Is a Dangerous Ideal

Last summer, Lavinia, who has suffered from eating disorders and manic depression since she was a child of eight, decided—having managed to maintain her weight at 10st 7lb [140 lbs.] (a healthy size 12) for a number of months—it was time to become anorexic once more.

"I don't know how anyone could say I looked nice at 10st 7lb," [140 lbs.] says Lavinia, who subsequently turned to her pro-ana

Several pro-eating-disorder Web sites have forums for girls and women to discuss which celebrities they would most want to look like. These generally include extremely thin stars such as Victoria Beckham.

acquaintances for support. "I was disgusting. I couldn't even fit my hands around my upper arm. I was covered in lard and fat everywhere. Every time I looked at pictures in magazines, I hated myself. I felt like a hippo in comparison to all the celebrities."

And there, of course, lies the danger in the idolisation of slender stars, such as Victoria Beckham and Nicole Richie, who are constantly splashed on the front of celebrity magazines.

"I love magazines that show before and after pictures of celebrities who've lost weight," says Lavinia. "Magazines such as *Heat* accuse them of being too skinny, but I think they look great. In pro-ana terms, we say 'they're "thinspiration." 'When I see those pictures, they make me feel really bad for being the weight I am. It motivates me to lose weight and be thinner. "I feel fat, I look fat and I am fat, so why would I settle for that? I would be much happier if I had a figure like Victoria Beckham's."

Dr. Dee Dawson, of the Rhodes Farm clinic in London, which specialises in eating disorders, says: "Mrs Beckham is usually the celebrity most people I see want to look like. She is horribly thin—you can see all her ribs—and she is not normal."

Anorexia Is Considered a Lifestyle Choice by Pro-ana Supporters

And yet still she is the kind of woman who appeals to young girls blighted by anorexia. One such victim is Katie Parker, 17, who lives with her father, an engineer, her mother, a musician and brother and sister in Wiltshire [England]. She, too, has turned to pro-anorexia Web sites for advice on how to reach her desired weight of 7st 4lb [102 lbs.].

"When I looked in the mirror, I hated what I saw," says Katie, a student, who has a history of eating disorders and extreme dieting, but is now on the road to recovery. My arms were too big and my stomach seemed to stick out. When I found the pro-ana websites after searching online, it made me feel as though I was a part of something instead of all alone.

I liked the fact anorexia was considered a lifestyle, not a disease, and I thought it was great that everyone was helping each other. I got all sorts of advice on things you can do to avoid eating and how to deal with hunger pangs.

I used to feel as though I was walking a tightrope where on one side I could become underweight and ill, and on the other I could become really fat. I used to see food as the enemy. But being pro-ana put me back in control. . . .

Pro-eating-disorder Web Sites Encourage Unhealthy Weight Loss

Within weeks of beginning her starvation diet, Lavinia, who constantly refers to herself as "fat", "ugly" and "a pig" found herself succumbing to headaches, weakness and blackouts.

"I quickly felt exhausted and found myself literally asleep at my desk," she says. "I was losing weight, but not enough, which made me feel disgusted about myself and hatred for my body. "There were times when I felt stuck and as though I'm a failed anorexic. I don't want to be ill for work, but all I want to do is lose weight and I'm quite willing to do whatever it takes."

And despite her claim to want to maintain a degree of good health, Lavinia admits that she can't resist competing with the girls at her local Eating Disorders Unit, which by horrible coincidence she has to walk past on her way to her counselling sessions. "I feel that if I'm not in there, or if I'm not seeing someone at that clinic, then obviously I'm a failure," she says. "I look at them and think about how thin they are, how flat their stomachs are and how loose their trousers are, and feel fat in comparison. I know it's daft, but that's the way I think." . . .

Fast Fact

A 2005 study by doctors based at the Lucille Packard Children's Hospital in Palo Alto, California, found that more than 60 percent of eating disorder patients who visited pro-ana sites learned weight-loss techniques from the sites.

Pro-eating-disorder Web Sites Make the Problem Worse

Deanne Jade, of the National Centre for Eating Disorders, is not suprised to hear about the plight of Lavinia and Katie, and calls pro-ana sites the "pornography of eating disorders". She blames such sites for glamorizing the condition. "There are sites that genuinely try to help people into recovery, and as anorexia is a very lonely illness, it can also be beneficial to meet others in the same place, but most are offering advice that is dangerous," she says.

"Pro-anorexia sites often plug into the very feelings that are keeping so many women trapped by the illness, such as the sense of feeling different from everyone else, or feeling powerful, or feeling freed from having to grow up and live a normal life,' says Deanne. 'It worries me greatly that these sites lead women to say "anorexia is my lifestyle choice". The truth of the matter is that anorexia is never anyone's choice, it's a compulsion.' Dr Dee Dawson, of Rhodes Farm, agrees. 'I think these pro-anorexia websites are disgraceful and I wish the internet servers would do more about them,' she says. 'They're not helpful for anybody, and are clearly detrimental, especially to the young, impressionable women. 'We know that about 10 per cent of women with anorexia die from it. People who continue life at these very low weights, believing them to be OK, will develop osteoporosis, will be infertile and have heart problems. Anorexic women, and men, do not lead long or happy lives. And these websites are only perpetuating the problem."

EVALUATING THE AUTHOR'S ARGUMENTS:

Natasha Courtenay-Smith quotes from several sources to support the points she makes in her essay. Make a list of everyone she quotes, including their credentials and the nature of their comments Then, analyze her sources—are they credible? Are they well qualified to speak on the subject?

Viewpoint 4

Pro-eating disorder Web Sites Offer Some Positive Support

Business Wire

"Teens visiting the pro-eating disorder sites were more likely to describe themselves as recovering from their disorder than were their peers who did not visit the sites."

In the following viewpoint, *Business Wire* argues that eating disorder sufferers can find support at pro-eating-disorder Web sites. While they admit that these Web sites can be harmful, a study showed that those who visit the sites are more likely to describe themselves as recovering from an eating disorder than peers who did not visit the sites. Researchers speculate that this is because those who suffer from eating disorders use the sites as a forum to express their innermost thoughts and feelings, and the peer support they receive enables them to move toward recovery. Sharing personal experience and struggles with eating disorders validates their experience and ultimately helps some members to help seek treatment and recovery options. *Business Wire* concludes that while thcse Web sites

Business Wire, "Web Sites Promoting Eating Disorders Are Widely Used by Adolescents with the Condition, Say Researchers at Stanford and Lucile Packard Children's Hospital," May 16, 2005. Reproduced by permission.

can serve both positive and negative purposes, they do ultimately offer strong peer support. *Business Wire* is a global distributor of commercial news.

AS YOU READ, CONSIDER THE FOLLOWING QUESTIONS:

1. What is the ratio of Web sites that promote eating disorders to Web sites dedicated to recovery?
2. How did the health of adolescents with eating disorders who visited pro-eating-disorder sites differ from those who didn't visit the sites?
3. How were teens more likely to describe themselves after visiting pro-eating-disorder sites?

Web sites that actively promote anorexia and bulimia are used by a significant number of adolescents with eating disorders, according to a [2005] study from the Stanford School of Medicine and Lucile Packard Children's Hospital (LPCH) researchers.

Health Effects of Pro-eating-disorder Web Sites

Visitors to these sites are using them to obtain tips on weight loss and how to hide their food avoidance tactics from friends and family members, the researchers say. The study also finds that these teens are spending less time on schoolwork than their peers and more time in the hospital than those who do not use the sites.

"This is the first study that begins to examine the health effects of frequenting these sites, which outnumber those dedicated to recovery by five to one," said Stanford's Jenny Wilson. Many of the sites are designed and maintained by teens or young adults with eating disorders.

"These Web sites are founded on the mistaken belief that eating disorders are not a disease, but a way of life," said LPCH adolescent medicine specialist Rebecka Peebles, MD. "They are well-designed and alluring, often with a gateway emphasizing the danger of the site that can be attractive to teens."

Peebles, who studies both eating disorders and obesity, and Wilson, a Stanford medical student, co-authored the research, which will be presented in poster format at the annual meeting of the Pediatric Academic Societies in Washington, D.C. on May 16. LPCH adolescent medicine specialist Iris Litt, MD, was the senior advisor for the work. Litt is the Marron and Mary Elizabeth Kendrick Professor in Pediatrics at the Stanford University School of Medicine and former editor-in-chief of the *Journal of Adolescent Health.*

Visitors of Sites Spend More Time in the Hospital

The research is the culmination of a preliminary study conducted through an anonymous survey of medical histories and internet use sent to the families of adolescents diagnosed with an eating disorder at LPCH since 1997. Patients and parents were asked to fill out separate forms documenting their struggles with the condition. Fifty-two adolescents and 77 parents responded.

Wilson and Peebles found that 40 percent of the adolescents who responded had visited Web sites promoting eating disorders, and 34 percent had visited sites dedicated to recovery from the condition. About one quarter frequented both types of sites, and half the respondents had visited neither. Parents of teens who visited the sites promoting the disorder were more likely to know about the sites and to be concerned about the information their child accessed online than were parents of non-users.

> **FAST FACT**
>
> **A May 2005 study by Stanford researchers found that 34 percent of adolescents with eating disorders have visited pro-recovery Web sites.**

Although adolescents who visited the pro-eating disorder sites reported spending less time on school work and more time in the hospital, they did not differ from those who didn't visit these sites in a number of other health measures: how their weight compared with their ideal body weight, the duration of their eating disorder, the number of missed menses and the presence or absence of osteoporosis.

Why Users Visit Pro-eating-disorder Sites

Anorexics and bulimics visit pro-eating-disorder Web sites primarily because they feel bad about themselves, need company, and are stressed, a 2007 study found.

Reasons for visiting	Percent answering "YES"
Do you regularly look at?	
Food information (calories, etc.)	60%
Exercise information	39%
Verbal "thinspirations"	46%
Picture "thinspirations"	59%
Tips and tricks	59%
Chat room/forum/message board	74%
Diversions/jokes/artwork	30%
Essays/poetry/other cultural/political content	38%
What motivates you to visit the sites?	
Feeling good about yourself	26%
Feeling bad about yourself	69%
Feeling stressed	50%
Boredom	37%
Need for information	46%
Need for company; to interact with others on the sites	52%

Taken from: Emise Csipke and Outi Horne, "Pro-Eating-Disorder Web Sites: Users' Opinions," *European Eating Disorders Review*, vol. 15, no. 3, May–June 2007, p. 200.

While the sites provide 'thinspiration' in the form of pictures, body weight goal charts, exercises and low-calorie recipes, they don't uniformly tout the perceived advantages of eating disorders.

Pro-eating-disorder Sites Can Promote Recovery

"There is a profound ambivalence that embodies the pro-eating-disorder sites," said Peebles. "There are discussions in chat rooms and on bulletin boards about how much the disorder pains sufferers and cautioning others against trying too hard to lose weight."

The researchers also found that about one quarter of those visiting sites intended to help teens recover from eating disorders actually learned about and tried new weight loss techniques or diet aids as a result of their visit. Of course, they learned similar tactics from sites promoting eating disorders: more than 60 percent of adolescents visiting those sites tried new techniques as a result.

The researchers' study underscores how dependent teens are on the Internet for health information and peer support. Adolescents typically use the sites promoting eating disorders as a forum to express their innermost thoughts and feelings, say the researchers. Perhaps as a result, teens visiting the pro-eating disorder sites were more likely to describe themselves as recovering from their disorder than were their peers who did not visit the sites.

"It's such a dichotomy," said Peebles. "Teens enter the sites promoting eating disorders possibly to gain solidarity and to express their pride in and publicize what they see as a lifestyle choice. At the same time they are cautioning others not to follow in their footsteps. Teens in the midst of an eating disorder need to voice what they want: to continue to lose weight. While many people believe the Web sites should be shut down, it could be a very isolating experience for the users."

The researchers caution that the results of this study are preliminary. They plan a larger, prospective study designed to more closely follow health outcomes in newly diagnosed eating disorder patients who visit the sites. But in the meantime, they hope their results will serve as a wake-up call for physicians treating adolescents with eating disorders, who may underestimate the influence the Web sites may be having on their patients.

Because teens use the Internet as a primary source for peer support and health information, sites with eating disorder content need to focus on healthy dieting and recovery.

"Medical professionals need to recognize the important role the Internet is playing in the education and mis-education of their patients," said Litt. "These websites offer peer group support, which can be used for good or for evil."

EVALUATING THE AUTHORS' ARGUMENTS:

In this viewpoint, the authors argue that pro-eating-disorder Web sites offer support to those suffering from eating disorders, providing a welcoming community where members can get help. How do you think each of the other authors in this chapter might respond to this suggestion? List each author and write two or three sentences on what you think their response might be.

Facts About Eating Disorders

Editors' note: These facts can be used in reports or papers to reinforce or add credibility when making important points or claims.

Ages of Eating Disorder Sufferers

According to Anorexia Nervosa and Related Eating Disorders, Inc. (ANRED):

- 70 percent of body dysmorphic disorder (BDD) sufferers are struck before age eighteen.
- One in four college-aged women has bulimia.
- The secrecy surrounding bulimia makes it difficult to quantify the number of older people who suffer from the disease.
- Bulimia is rare in young children.
- Though anorexia and bulimia mainly affect people in their teens and twenties, studies report both disorders in kids as young as six years old and in people as old as seventy-six.

The National Association of Anorexia Nervosa and Associated Disorders has found that:

- 86 percent of eating disorder sufferers report onset of illness by twenty years old.
- 10 percent report onset of an eating disorder at ten years old or younger.
- 33 percent report onset of an eating disorder between the ages of eleven and fifteen.
- 43 percent report onset of an eating disorder between the ages of sixteen and twenty.

Eating Disorders and Mental Illness and Substance Abuse

According to the National Institute of Mental Health:

- Eating disorders are often accompanied by other psychiatric conditions, such as depression, substance abuse, or anxiety disorders.
- Studies show that antidepressants may not prevent those with anorexia from experiencing relapses.

- Some studies indicate greater success for weight gain and mood elevation when parents take on the responsibility for feeding their anorexic adolescent.
- People who are obese and are diagnosed with binge-eating disorder often also suffer from depression, anxiety, and personality disorders.

According to ANRED:

- Approximately 72 percent of female alcoholics who are younger than thirty years old also suffer from an eating disorder.
- Many people who suffer from eating disorders also abuse drugs.

Men and Boys with Eating Disorders

According to the National Institute of Mental Health:

- Men and boys make up approximately 5 to 15 percent of those with anorexia or bulimia.
- Thirty-five percent of men and boys who suffer from anorexia or bulimia also have binge-eating disorder.
- One out of four preteen patients with anorexia is male, while binge-eating disorder affects girls and boys at about the same rates.

ANRED has found that about 10 percent of those with anorexia and bulimia are male.

The National Association of Anorexia Nervosa and Associated Disorders says that approximately 1 million American men suffer from an eating disorder.

Body dysmorphic disorder (BDD) affects around 2 percent of Americans—affecting males and females equally, according to ANRED.

The Academy for Eating Disorders has found that men and boys who participate in sports such as wrestling, bodybuilding, crew, running, football, and cycling face an increased risk for developing an eating disorder.

Women and Girls with Eating Disorders

According to the National Association of Anorexia Nervosa and Associated Disorders, about 7 million women suffer from an eating disorder.

According to the Academy for Eating Disorders:

- Anorexia among young women is as common as autism.
- Between 1 and 3 percent of young women suffer from bulimia.
- Between 4 and 20 percent of females have unhealthy dieting, bingeing, and purging habits.
- Female athletes such as gymnasts, ice skaters, dancers, and swimmers are prone to eating disorders.
- Thirty-three percent of female Division 1 NCAA athletes reported attitudes or symptoms that put them at risk for developing anorexia.
- White females may be more likely to suffer from anorexia nervosa.
- African American females may be more vulnerable to binge-eating disorders.
- Body dissatisfaction in young girls affects white, African American, Hispanic, and Asian girls.
- Around .5 to 1 percent of late teens or adult women meet criteria for an anorexia diagnosis.
- Approximately 1 to 2 percent of late teens and adult women meet criteria for a bulimia diagnosis.
- At least 10 percent of late teens and adult women report eating disorder symptoms.

According to SomethingFishy.org, the average female model weighs up to 25 percent less than the average woman.

According to ANRED:

- Women are at 3 times greater risk for developing an eating disorder than men.
- The average woman is 5 feet, 4 inches tall, weighs 145 pounds, wears a size 11 to 14 dress, and has hips that measure 40 to 42 inches around.
- If Barbie was real she would be 6 feet tall, weigh 101 pounds, wear a size 4 dress, and her hips would measure just 33 inches around.
- Research indicates that approximately 1 percent of women in the United States have binge-eating disorder.

Treatment, Outlook, and Consequences

According to the National Institute of Mental Health:

- People who suffer from anorexia may be up to 10 times more likely to die as a result of their illness than those without the disorder.
- Neuroimaging, such as magnetic resonance imaging (MRI), may give important clues about eating disorders.
- The death rate among those who suffer from anorexia is approximately .56 percent annually. This is about twelve times higher than the annual mortality rate from all causes of death among females between the ages of fifteen and twenty-four.
- The mortality rate increases up to 20 percent for those who suffer from anorexia for more than twenty years.

According to ANRED:

- Up to 20 percent of those with serious eating disorders die without treatment.
- With treatment, that number falls to about 2 or 3 percent.
- Around 60 percent of people with eating disorders recover with treatment.
- Approximately 20 percent of people with eating disorders who get treatment make only partial recoveries.
- Twenty percent of people who suffer from eating disorders do not improve even with treatment.
- Recovery takes on average from five to seven years.

According to the National Association of Anorexia Nervosa and Associated Disorders:

- Inpatient treatment for an eating disorder may cost $30,000 or more a month.
- Outpatient treatment may cost $100,000 or more.
- Seventy-seven percent of people report suffering from an eating disorder from 1 to 15 years, 30 percent from 1 to 5 years, 31 percent for 6 to 10 years, and 16 percent report suffering for 11 to 15 years.
- Approximately 6 percent of serious eating disorder patients will die.
- Around 50 percent of sufferers report reaching full recovery.

According to the Academy for Eating Disorders:

- Up to 10 percent of women with anorexia may die from causes related to the disease.
- Risk of death among people who suffer from anorexia is twelve times higher than for those the same age without anorexia.
- Anorexia has lifelong health consequences such as osteoporosis, gastrointestinal complications, and dental problems.
- Approximately 50 percent of those with anorexia recover. Thirty-three percent of patients with anorexia experience partial recovery, and 20 percent remain chronically ill.
- Approximately 50 percent of those who are bulimic recover. Thirty percent of bulimic patients see a partial recovery, and 20 percent continue to meet full criteria for bulimia.
- Long-term studies show that only 10 percent of bulimic people continue to fully meet bulimic criteria after 10 years. Evidence suggests that cognitive behavioral therapy may speed up recovery for those who suffer from bulimia.

Organizations to Contact

The editors have compiled the following list of organizations concerned with the issues debated in this book. The descriptions are derived from materials provided by the organizations. All have publications or information available for interested readers. The list was compiled on the date of publication of the present volume; the information provided here may change. Be aware that many organizations take several weeks or longer to respond to inquiries, so allow as much time as possible.

Academy for Eating Disorders (AED)

111 Deer Lake Rd., Ste. 100
Deerfield, IL 60015
(847) 498-4274
Web site: www.aedweb.org

The Academy for Eating Disorders (AED) is a global, multidisciplinary professional organization that provides cutting-edge professional training and education; inspires new developments in eating disorders research, prevention, and clinical treatments; and is the international source for state-of-the-art information in the field of eating disorders.

Alliance for Eating Disorders Awareness

PO Box 13155
North Palm Beach, FL 33408-3133
(866) 662-1235
e-mail: info@eatingdisorderinfo.org
Web site: www.aedweb.org

This organization seeks to establish easily accessible programs across the nation that allow children and young adults the opportunity to learn about eating disorders and the positive effects of a healthy body image. Its aim is to disseminate educational information to parents and caregivers about the warning signs, dangers, and consequences of anorexia, bulimia, and other related disorders.

American Psychiatric Association (APA)

1000 Wilson Blvd., Ste. 1825
Arlington, VA 22209-3901
(703) 907-7300
e-mail: apa@psych.org
Web site: www.psych.org

APA is an organization of psychiatrists dedicated to studying the nature, treatment, and prevention of mental disorders, including those that contribute to eating disorders. It helps create mental health policies, distributes information about psychiatry, and promotes psychiatric research and education.

American Psychological Association (APA)

750 First St. NE
Washington, DC 20002-4242
(202) 336-5500 • (800) 374-2721
e-mail: public.affairs@apa.org
Web site: www.apa.org

This scientific and professional organization represents psychology in the United States. With 150,000 members, the APA is the largest association of psychologists worldwide. It produces numerous publications on eating disorders and other topics related to psychology.

Anorexia Nervosa and Related Eating Disorders, Inc. (ANRED)

PO Box 5102
Eugene, OR 97405
(503) 344-1144
Web site: www.anred.com

ANRED is a nonprofit organization that provides information about anorexia nervosa, bulimia nervosa, binge-eating disorder, compulsive exercising, and other lesser-known food and weight disorders, including details about recovery and prevention. ANRED offers workshops, individual and professional training, as well as local community education. It also produces a monthly newsletter.

The Center for the Study of Anorexia and Bulimia

1841 Broadway, 4th Flr.
New York, NY 10023

(212) 333-3444
e-mail: csab@icpnyc.org
Web site: http://csabnyc.org

CSAB is the oldest nonprofit eating disorders clinic in New York City, devoted to treating individuals with eating disorders and training the professionals who work with them.

Eating Disorders Awareness and Prevention, Inc. (EDAP)

603 Stewart St., Ste. 803
Seattle, WA 98101
(206) 382-3587 • Toll-free Information and Referral Helpline: (800) 931-2237
e-mail: info@NationalEatingDisorders.org
Web site: www.edap.org

EDAP is dedicated to promoting the awareness and prevention of eating disorders by encouraging positive self-esteem and size acceptance. It provides free and low-cost educational information on eating disorders and their prevention. EDAP also provides educational outreach programs and training for schools and universities and sponsors the Puppet Project for Schools and the annual National Eating Disorders Awareness Week. EDAP publishes a prevention curriculum for grades four through six as well as public prevention and awareness information packets, videos, guides, and other materials.

Eating Disorders Coalition for Research, Policy and Action

611 Pennsylvania Ave. SE, #423
Washington, DC 20003-4303
(202) 543-9570
fax: (202) 543-9570
Web site: www.eatingdisorderscoalition.org

The mission of the Eating Disorders Coalition for Research, Policy and Action is to advance the federal recognition of eating disorders as a public health priority.

Harvard Eating Disorders Center (HEDC)

356 Boylston St.
Boston, MA 02118

(888) 236-1188
Web site: www.hedc.org

HEDC is a national nonprofit organization dedicated to advancing the field of eating disorders through research, training, education, and outreach. It works to expand knowledge about eating disorders and their detection, treatment, and prevention and promotes the healthy development of women, children, and everyone at risk. A primary goal for the organization is lobbying for health policy initiatives on behalf of individuals with eating disorders.

National Association of Anorexia and Associated Disorders (ANAD)

Box 7
Highland Park, IL 60035
(847) 831-3438
Web site: www.anad.org

ANAD offers hot-line counseling, operates an international network of support groups for people with eating disorders and their families, and provides referrals to health-care professionals who treat eating disorders. It produces a quarterly newsletter and information packets and organizes national conferences and local programs. All ANAD services are provided free of charge.

National Eating Disorder Information Centre (NEDIC)

ES 7-421, 200 Elizabeth St., M5G 2C4
Toronto, ON M5G 2C4, CANADA
(1-866) NEDIC-20 (1-866) 633-4220
e-mail: nedic@uhn.on.ca
Web site: www.nedic.ca/index.shtml

NEDIC is a Toronto-based organization that provides information and resources on eating disorders and weight preoccupation. It focuses on the sociocultural factors that influence female health-related behaviors. NEDIC promotes healthy lifestyles and encourages individuals to make informed choices based on accurate information. It publishes a newsletter and a guide for families and friends of eating-disorder sufferers and sponsors Eating Disorders Awareness Week in Canada.

Society for Adolescent Medicine (SAM)
1916 NW Copper Oaks Circle
Blue Springs, MO 64015
(816) 224-8010
Web site: www.adolescenthealth.org

SAM is a multidisciplinary organization of professionals committed to improving the physical and psychosocial health and well-being of all adolescents. It helps plan and coordinate national and international professional education programs on adolescent health. Its publications include the monthly *Journal of Adolescent Health* and the quarterly *SAM Newsletter.*

For Further Reading

Books

De Pree, Julia K. *Body Story*. Athens, OH: Swallow Press/Ohio University Press, 2004. The memoir of a woman who developed a life-threatening eating disorder at the age of thirteen and her subsequent struggles.

Gura, Trisha. *Lying in Weight: The Hidden Epidemic of Eating Disorders in Adult Women*. New York: HarperCollins, May 2007. Suggests there exist millions of uncounted people who suffer from disordered eating and other "subthreshold" eating disorders.

Lucas, Alexander R. *Demystifying Anorexia Nervosa: An Optimistic Guide to Understanding and Healing*. New York: Oxford University Press, 2008. Offers clear guidance and authoritative advice on how to overcome anorexia nervosa. Based on a physician's unique research with thousands of patients.

Mendelsohn, Susan J. *It's Not About the Weight: Attacking Eating Disorders from the Inside Out*, iUniverse, 2007. Part self-help guide and part memoir, this book tackles growing up with—and growing through—the challenge of body image distortions.

Strober, Michael A. and Meg F. Schneider, *Just a Little Too Thin: How to Pull Your Child Back from the Brink of an Eating Disorder*. Cambridge, MA: Da Capo, 2006. A thorough and informative guide that targets teens who are teetering on the edge of a potential eating disorder, exhibiting warning signs yet still on the brink.

Periodicals

Courtenay-Smith, Natasha. "The Cult of Anorexia," *Daily Mail* (United Kingdom), June 29, 2006. www.dailymail.co.uk/pages/live/fcmail/article.html?in_article_id=393037&in_page_id=1879.

Csipke, Emese, and Outi Horne. "Pro-eating-disorder Web Sites: Users' Opinions," *European Eating Disorders Review*, vol. 15, no. 3, May/June 2007.

Faiad, Andrea. "Dying to Be Thin: Eating Disorders Are Ugly. Here's Why," *Current Health* 2, November 2006.

Goodchild, Sophie. "Dying to Be Thin," AlterNet.com, November 22, 2006. www.alternet.org/story/44526/?page=1.

Graham, Lacey. "The Myth of the Ideal Female Body," *Reno News and Review,* November 2003. www.newsreview.com/reno/Content?oid=21357.

Guernsey, Diane. "One Family's Nightmare: A Teenager Is Emaciated. Her Parents Feel Powerless, What Next?" *Town & Country,* April 2006.

Head, Jacqueline. "Seeking 'Thinspiration,'" BBC.com, August 8. 2007. http://news.bbc.co.uk/l/hi/magazine/6935768.stm.

Hughes, Zondra. "Dying to Be Thin: Deadly Eating Disorders Are Killing Some Sisters Who Are Desperately Trying to Control Their Weight," *Ebony,* July 2005.

Johnston, Jenifer. "Revealed: Experts' Fears over Craze for Anorexic Web Sites HEALTH:" *Sunday Herald,* July 9, 2006.

Klein, Sarah. "Through Thick and Thin: Pro Eating Disorder Web Sites Still Going Strong," *Metro Times* (Detroit), March 30. 2005. www.metrotimes.com/editorial/story.asp?id=7499.

Nagourney, Eric. "Web Sites Celebrate a Deadly Thinness," *New York Times,* June 7, 2005. www.nytimes.com/2005/06/07/health/nutrition/07eat.html?pagewanted=2.

National Institute of Mental Health. "Eating Disorders," 2007. www.nimh.nih.gov/health/publications/eating-disorders/nimheating disorders.pdf.

Norris, Mark L, Katherine M. Boydell, Leora Pinhas, and Debra K. Katzman. "Ana and the Internet: A Review of Pro-anorexia Web Sites," vol. 39, no. 6, *International Journal of Eating Disorders,* September 2006.

Rankman, Angie. "Pro-ana: *Still* Dying to Be Thin," *Aphrodite Women's Health,* June 12, 2006. www.aphroditewomenshealth.com/news/pro-ana.shtml.

Santa Lucia, Lynn. "Driven to Be Thin: Millions of Teens Suffer from Eating Disorders and Many of Them Are Boys," *Scholastic Choices,* September 2006.

Schwirzer, Jennifer. "Drop Dead Beautiful: Part 1: Food Fuels Our Lives. But for Some, It Becomes a Tool of Self-Destruction, *Vibrant Life*, September/October 2005.

Semuels, Alana. "Thin Girls Online: Web Sites That Advocate Eating Disorders Worry Health Experts," *Pittsburgh Post-Gazette*, June 22, 2005. www.post-gazette.com/pg/05173/525994.stm.

Springen, Karen. "The Dangers of Pro-anorexia Web Sites: Mixed Messages," *Newsweek*, December 7, 2006. www.newsweek.com/id/44107.

Weaver, Clair. "Internet Encourages Eating Disorders," *Daily Telegraph* (Australia), September 2, 2007. www.news.com.au/dailytelegraph/story/0,22049.22346309500 1021,00.html.

Web Sites

Body Image Health (www.bodyimagehealth.org). This Web site confronts two of today's greatest health and wellness concerns—the drive to be thin and the rising rate of fatness—providing a new approach to prevent body image problems in adults and children before they start.

Eating Disorder Referral and Information Center (www.edreferral.com). Provides information and treatment resources for all types of eating disorders. Offers eating disorder victims help finding medical professionals.

Eating Disorders Anonymous (www.eatingdisordersanonymous.org). This is a Web site for a twelve-step self-help group for anorexics and bulimics. It has links to meetings and discussion boards that eating disorder sufferers will find interesting and useful.

Eating Disorders Association (EDA) (www.edauk.com). A British Web site containing information on aspects of eating disorders including anorexia nervosa, bulimia nervosa, binge-eating disorder and related eating disorders.

EDEN: Eating Disordersand Education Network (www.edenclub.org). This is the Web site of a nonprofit organization designed to support individuals seeking recovery from eating and body image disorders. Its programs include a seventeen-week recovery program and a peer counseling program.

We Bite Back (www.webiteback.com). This Web site was started by a former moderator of a pro-ana site who realized such sites encouraged women to perpetuate their disease problem. Upon this realization, she started We Bite Back, which is a pro-recovery eating disorder Web site.

Index

Picture Credits

Maury Aaseng, 14, 19, 27, 32, 40, 48, 54, 83, 94, 114
AP Images, 25
Associated Prcss, 96
© Bubbles Photolibrary/Alamy, 10, 13, 37, 64, 102
Business Wire via Getty Images, 43
Cartoon by Dan Rosandich. www.CartoonStock.com, 100
Chicago/PA photos/Landov, 107
Fotos International/Hulton Archive/Getty Images, 86
© ImageState/Alamy, 35
Lisa Marcelja/Maxppp/Landov, 90
© Photofusion Picture Library/Alamy, 20
© Photo Network/Alamy, 57
© Picture Partners/Alamy, 77, 116
© Frances M. Roberts/Alamy, 47
© 2006 by Mike Keefe and CagleCartoons.com. All rights reserved, 68
Maria Jose Zubillaga/Reuters/Landov, 71

About The Editors

Lauri S. Friedman earned her bachelor's degree in religion and political science from Vassar College in 1999. Her studies there focused on political Islam, and she produced a thesis on the Islamic Revolution in Iran titled *Neither West, Nor East, but Islam.* She also holds a preparatory degree in flute performance from the Manhattan School of Music.

She is the founder of LSF Editorial, a writing and editing outfit in San Diego, CA. Her clients include Greenhaven Press, for whom she has edited numerous titles on gay marriage, drug abuse, the war on terror, Iraq, pandemics, genetic engineering, and more. A former in-house senior editor at Greenhaven, she helped conceive of and design the *Introducing Issues with Opposing Viewpoints* series.

Friedman lives in Ocean Beach, San Diego, with her husband, Randy, and their yellow lab, Trucker. In her spare time she enjoys pottery, making music, taking Trucker to the beach, and traveling.

Jennifer L. Skancke lives and works in San Francisco. Aside from writing, she loves reading, HBO programming, learning Italian, hiking, camping, traveling, and laughing with friends.